The Lost Seigneur

"*The Lost Seigneur* is David Loux's second novel about the du Laux family, in which the story of its patriarch, Jean-Pierre du Laux, unfolds . . . Mr. Loux has rendered with fine strokes, the story of a family, and the forces in the Old World and the New that shaped it."
MARYELLEN BEVERIDGE, AUTHOR, *PERMEABLE BOUNDARIES*

"*The Lost Seigneur: A Château Laux Odyssey* by David Loux is a mesmerising journey that ensnares readers right from the opening line, drawing them into a meticulously crafted tale of emotional depth. . . . This captivating story unfolds the delicate dance between loss and redemption, illuminating the beauty found in mending what has been broken."
MARY ANNE YARDE, *COFFEE POT BOOK CLUB*

"It is a hauntingly beautiful story of grief, tenacity, and silent triumph that is written with elegance, historical accuracy, and emotional depth."
HISTORICAL FICTION COMPANY

"*The Lost Seigneur* is a sweeping historical fiction that digs deep into faith and family, love and loss, while telling a heartwarming tale of people coming together not only to survive but to thrive against challenging odds."
BOOKLIFE REVIEWS BY *PUBLISHER'S WEEKLY* (EDITOR'S PICK)

"*The Lost Seigneur* is a touching and well-told journey about loss, love, and finding your way back. If you enjoy stories that are both personal and historical, this one is well worth your time."
THE BOOK ADDICT

"In David Loux's sequel, *The Lost Seigneur*, to his award-winning first novel, Chateau Laux, the reader is again rewarded with exquisite writing, a finely plotted story and immersion into a family saga of love, loyalty, tragedy and triumph."
BARBARA STARK-NEMON, AUTHOR OF *EVEN IN DARKNESS, HARD CIDER,* AND *ISABELLA'S WAY*

"This is a family saga about profound personal loss, courage and resilience, and discovering hope and love. I highly recommend David Loux's *The Lost Seigneur . . .*"
READERS' FAVORITE

"An emotionally intense drama with a satisfying, unexpected conclusion."
KIRKUS REVIEWS

"A lush, historical novel."
FOREWORD CLARION REVIEWS

"Loved it!"
REEDSY DISCOVERY

THE LOST SEIGNEUR

THE LOST SEIGNEUR

A CHATEAU LAUX ODYSSEY

DAVID LOUX

Wire Gate Press

RENO, NV

The Lost Seigneur
BY David Loux

© 2025 by David Loux

Although this work was inspired by an actual past event, this is a work of fiction. Names, characters, businesses, places, events, and incidents are either the products of the author's imaginations or used in a fictitious manner. Any resemblance to actual persons, living or dead, or actual events is purely coincidental.

ISBN 978-1-954065-04-8 (trade paperback original)
ISBN 978-1-954065-03-1 (Epub)
Library of Congress Control Number: 2025939090

Publication Date: October 7, 2025

BISAC category code
FIC019000 FICTION/Literary
FIC014070 FICTION/Historical/Colonial America & Revolution
FIC008000 FICTION/Sagas
FIC051000 FICTION/Cultural Heritage

First Edition

COVER DESIGN AND INTERIOR DESIGN:
KG Design International; kgeokat@gmail.com

Wire Gate Press
Reno, NV
wiregatepress@gmail.com

Hasard [ʻazar]
French: chance, coincidence
According to some, the mantle of God, and the footprints
that he leaves in the world

THE LOST SEIGNEUR

The origin of the Cathar faith is not known with absolute certainty. Many historians trace its roots to the Byzantine Empire, from where it most likely traveled through the Balkans and arrived in Europe along with the early crusaders returning from the Levant. It was a dualistic faith, grounded in Christian Gnosticism, which clashed with traditional Roman Catholicism.

By 1143, the Cathars were firmly entrenched in southern France. They had their own church structure, with bishops in Albi, Toulouse, Carcassonne and Agen. Cathar adepts freely wandered the countryside, administering the duties of their faith. One of the things that set Catharism apart from its Roman counterpart was that women were considered coequal with men. Many noble families had mothers and sisters who were Cathars.

In response to this competitive threat, the Papacy instituted an inquisition against the Cathars in 1184. A full-blown military crusade against them followed in 1209. The Protestant Reformation introduced new threats to Rome, and the ensuing Wars of Religion continued the onslaught of one Christian group against another. These wars ended with the Edict of Nantes in 1598, which granted some religious toleration to Protestants. But French King Louis XIV instituted the Dragonnades in 1681, which billeted troops in the homes of Protestants, in an attempt to force their conversion to Catholicism. Atrocities were commonplace.

Jean-Pierre's story takes place in the waning years of the seven-teenth century and the decades that followed, in a land that suffered a persistent legacy of religious turmoil.

The afternoon turned the worn hue of an old silver coin as Magdalena began the daily ritual of closing up the lonely château, which sat on a plot of cultivated land in the new-world colony of Penn's Woods, not far from the western frontier. First, she checked the bolt on the front door as well as the one that led from the mudroom to her husband's vineyard. Then she pulled the heavy drapes on the long windows, shutting out the meadow views on one side of the house and the distant line of oak forest on the other. The house was now in deep gloom, and she lit the lamps in the great room, where she intended to sit in front of the unlit fireplace and await the further advance of the coming night.

Before settling down with her book, however, she tidied up the kitchen. The iron skillet needed to be scrubbed and her plate and single setting of silverware washed. Her husband, Lawrence, had installed a drain in the sink—it was one of the little improvements he was always coming up with—and she poured the wastewater away while the dishes air-dried on a tea towel. Then, satisfied that all was in order at last, she retired to her waiting chair.

The château had two stories, and the upper level loomed with a presence that was not quite ominous. In the winters, the upstairs became so frigid that water froze in the glass by the bedside. Now, however, the summer heat gathered like a woolen blanket, making her feel hot and itchy. As a distraction from thinking about the upstairs furnace lying in wait, she usually read until fatigue crept over her with enough force that sleep would beckon. Remus had no problem getting comfortable wherever he happened to be, she thought, her gaze stealing to the mastiff at her feet. Magdalena's father had given her the dog as a puppy on her wedding day, and now, at three years old, it lay with its jowly head on her foot, reassuring her with its company.

A sudden knock on the door startled her. Remus picked up his head and gave a throaty woof. Setting her book aside, Magdalena rose and made her way to the foyer, the dog padding at her side.

"Who is it?" she called out.

"It's the post, ma'am—from the stage depot," a youthful voice piped, and Remus issued a low growl. After the death of his first wife, Catharine, who had been Magdalena's older sister, Lawrence was loath to leave her alone. But he was in the Pennsylvania assembly now, which met in Philadelphia, a two-day ride away. He had wanted Magdalena to accompany him. But while she was glad to be out of her mother's house, she couldn't stand the thought of being too far removed, either, which meant that during her husband's absences, the post was their only means of keeping in touch.

A young man stood on the threshold, his face glowing in the lamplight. Behind him, where his horse patiently waited, the last silvern vestiges of the waning day had given way to the creeping purples of twilight. The cicadas were particularly loud this year, and the coming night seemed to drive them into a frenzy. Their thundering chorus made it hard even to think.

"Thank you," Magdalena said, accepting the letter the young postman withdrew from the leather pouch that hung around his neck. The lad beamed when she dropped a couple of coins in his palm, and waved cheerfully as he turned away.

After climbing up onto his horse, he waved again, and Remus let out another growl.

"Oh, calm down, you," Magdalena said, glancing affectionately at her companion as she shut the door and rebolted it. The dog looked up at her, his eyes rolling, and she reached down and scratched behind his ear.

Heading into the kitchen, she placed the letter on the oversized wooden table and lit the lamp that sat on the counter. Visitors to the château were not unwelcome, but they created a disturbance like a draft on the neck—or were she more like Remus, hair rubbed the wrong way. It was an agitation that she didn't want to take into the great room, where her book waited. So, she placed a kettle on the heating plate of the kitchen hearth and added a couple more sticks of kindling underneath. She assumed the letter was from her husband and felt the tingle of suspense.

Once the water in the kettle had warmed, she poured a mug and added an infuser of tea leaves. She opened the letter with a knife from the block on the counter, then sat down rather ceremoniously at the table.

The letter was written in an unfamiliar longhand. It took time to read. Without thinking, she had placed the kettle back on the heating plate and it started to bubble and spit. Her hand began to shake. She read the letter again and yet a third time before lowering it to the table and staring into space.

◆ ◆ ◆

THE FOLLOWING MORNING, SHE WAS already awake when the sun first peeked over the heavily forested ridge to the east. The night had seemed endless, with the thunder of the cicadas and the creaks and moans of the house. With only a bedsheet for cover, because of the heat, she had lain on one side and then the other, then on her back and on her stomach, before turning once again. There were times she feared she wouldn't be able to sleep at all, and other times when she would awaken and stare up through the cloaking darkness with her eyes wide open. Finally, as the room began to brighten, she was relieved that she could put the long, miserable night behind her.

She was the kind of person who was rarely hungry in the morning. But the day ahead crowded her mind and she forced herself to eat some toast. Remus whined to be fed, wagging his heavy tail and peering up at her. As a self-professed Cathar, Magdalena did not eat meat, but that restriction did not apply to her husband and certainly not to her dog, and she sautéed a portion of venison shoulder just enough to singe it before spooning it into the bowl.

She had no problem finding the horse in the pasture and slipping a halter over its head to lead it to the barn. The grass was heavy with dew and after a few strides, her dress was soaked to the knees. The horse was compliant, and as they walked, it would lower its head and nibble at her in quest of a snack. This Magdalena blamed on her husband, who carried sugar lumps in his pocket. The sugar was from the Caribbean, which seemed a long way to come to end up in the belly of a horse.

Up at the barn, Magdalena curried the animal's hide with sweeping circular motions, then she fluffed off the dander with a brush. A horse's mane was forever getting tangled and she combed this as well before hitching the horse up to the wagon. One of her father's sayings was that if you wanted a friend, a good horse was hard to beat, and while Magdalena didn't always share every sentiment that he expressed, she loved his sayings nevertheless, for they were so many pieces of the whole that made up the man. Each of his sayings and kind observations were like a brick in one of the new red homes in nearby Watertown, individually of no consequence, perhaps, but in their accumulation something solid and real.

On the way to the farm where Magdalena had grown up, Remus loped ahead, scaring up robins and meadowlarks from the bordering fence line. The road cut through fields of rye and Indian maize, the wild, dark forest giving up here and receding there until it had grown more and more distant.

When they got to the Laux farm, Remus charged forward to greet his littermate, another equally imposing mastiff, and the two of them romped and rolled in the grass in front of the farmhouse. Magdalena parked the wagon at the wire gate next to the yard. Her mother, Beatrice, was in the kitchen, shaving carrot peels into a ceramic bowl on the counter. Beatrice wore a white apron over a gray linen dress with a pattern like the plumage of guinea fowl. She had on the wooden shoes she liked to wear in the kitchen.

"Hello, Mother," Magdalena said, which sounded a bit formal even to her. But that was the way she felt about her mother. There was a stiffness between them that did not exclude love, but which tended to put a damper on any unprovoked displays of warmth.

"If you've come to lend a hand with the peeling, I'm almost done," Beatrice blustered, and Magdalena smiled. It was a constant tease between them that she tended to show up at the farm just as a task neared completion.

"I hate to disappoint you . . ." she said.

"Then it must be your husband, kicking you out for good, this time."

Magdalena laughed.

"Mother, we've talked about this many times. Just because Lawrence has to spend at least some of his time in Philadelphia doesn't mean we're not happily married. It's an arrangement that suits us both."

Beatrice gave her head a shake, as if a husband and wife in a celibate marriage were something she simply could not comprehend. She had never made a secret of how she felt toward the Cathar women who had come to the farm when Magdalena was a child and somehow wormed their way into the little girl's affection. The women said that Magdalena was the image of her grandmother, who had been a Cathar *parfaite,* and while Beatrice was careful about what she said regarding her husband's mother, she had never held back when it came to perfect strangers putting their ideas into little Maggy's head.

"If it's your father you want, he'll be in the barn getting the cider press ready," she relented, scraping her carrot a little harder. "He wants to start appling next week, if your brother Georgie is done with his fever by then. Lord willing, no one else will get sick! One of Georgie's little ones already has the sniffles," she added, with an aggrieved sigh.

Magdalena had three older brothers, and Georgie, who had never once wanted to leave the farm and couldn't be happier living with his parents, shared his old bedroom with his wife, Rachel. Magdalena's oldest brother, Jean, was an officer in the Royal Navy. His room had gone to Georgie's son, Georgie Junior, and Magdalena's second brother, Andrew, owned a house of his own near one of the sawmills he ran, which left his room to Georgie's daughter, Sofie.

As if on cue, a boy of seven burst through the kitchen, clutching a corncob doll. A younger girl was in hot pursuit, her face beet red. "It's mine! Gimme it back!" she howled. The both of them bolted out through the kitchen door and Magdalena heard their voices receding into the yard.

"Give it to me!"

"Make me!"

"I see Georgie Junior takes after his father," Magdalena observed, wryly, referring to Georgie Senior, who as a child, himself, had always been ready to yank on a hair ribbon or pull a frog from his pocket.

Beatrice made an obvious effort not to retort, and Magdalena followed the children out onto the porch. Slipping past the tussling pair and the dogs that growled and wrestled in the yard, she headed out the wire gate and down the gravel path to the barn. She found her father, Pierre, in the cider room, as Beatrice had said, crouched in front of the apple press. Dipping a rag into a bucket of vinegar water, he carefully wiped at the flat surfaces and dabbed into the places that were hard to reach. Having oiled the press this past winter, he just had to remove the dust and then soak the wood so that it swelled and held the apple juice that spilled from the pulp bucket.

"Papa," she said, affectionately, inhaling the sweet, lingering odor of apple nectar that still perfumed the air from previous years.

Pierre looked up. He dropped the rag into the bucket of vinegar water.

"Daughter," he said, with a nod, and Magdalena nearly burst into tears. She loved it when he called her that. It reminded her anew that she had a place in his life and in his heart.

Thrusting the letter out, she waited while her father looked down at it. Pierre was a big man, which made the little things he did seem methodical, even such a thing as reading. His eyes seemed to fasten on one word and then move excruciatingly to the next, and Magdalena felt a bead of perspiration work its way past her ear and crawl down her neck. The stifling heat of the loft made her nose burn and her throat grew parched.

Finally, Pierre raised his head. But he was looking somewhere just past her and seemed to have a hard time focusing.

"What do you think?" she asked, at last, with a trembling voice. The letter was from the governor of Antigua, warning that a ship bound for La Florida had blown off course, with a man aboard who claimed to be Pierre's father. It said the seigneur had a daughter, whom the governor apparently found to be most disagreeable—too cunning for the fairer sex, as he put it—but that he nevertheless was doing everything in his power to expedite their passage to Philadelphia.

Pierre shook his head. Or maybe it just seemed like he moved it, Magdalena couldn't be sure.

"I don't understand," he said. "My parents are both gone. I laid my mother to rest with my own hands and my father disappeared when I was thirteen."

His shoulders sagged. For a moment, he stared down at the apple press as if struggling to remember what it was for. His knees buckled and he hobbled from the cider room to sit on the bench outside. With his shoulders hunched and the colonial sun on his face, he gazed at the far horizon as if waiting for something to materialize.

Magdalena sat down beside him.

"Papa?" she said, but he seemed not to hear.

"Papa, talk to me," she pleaded.

But for the first time in her life, she felt alone, even with the man she adored. As father and daughter, they shared a lot in common. But they were born on different continents and came from different worlds. He was born to privilege and she to stories of the loss of it, and sitting so close she could feel the heat of his body, she realized that there was much about him that she still did not know.

TWO

Well before Magdalena was born and had lived long enough to worry about such things as a husband who commuted to Philadelphia and, in his absence, how to get along in an empty house, a *mistral* whipped along the bluffs above a *manoir* in southern France. This dry, cold wind blew from the north, cutting through the Pyrenean foothills on its way to the Mediterranean. A devil wind, Jean-Pierre's mother used to call it, as if a wind could have a heart and soul and enough prescience to set its own course. Jean-Pierre was a seigneur, which meant he had feudal oversight of ancestral lands and the people who lived on them. In addition to his seigneurial duties, he attended the king's court, which meant he took frequent trips to Versailles, where he mingled with the Sun King and the other nobles. He was also a father and for the moment, at least, he watched his son, Pierre, ranging ahead of him on the bluffs, the sleeves of his cloak flapping.

The lad was next in a line of succession that went back hundreds of years. The land he now romped on in such a carefree manner would be his someday, as would the village in the river valley below, when he, in his turn, assumed the title of seigneur, and Jean-Pierre's chest swelled with pride. He congratulated himself for serving his forebears well by siring such a strong and forthright soul.

By now, the boy had reached the top of the bluff, and Jean-Pierre raised his fingers to his lips and whistled. The wind whipped the sound away, but it didn't matter, because the boy had already turned and was looking back at him. Jean-Pierre waved. The boy thrust his hands into his pockets and hunched his shoulders, leaning into the wind as he returned to his father's side.

Jean-Pierre clapped a hand on the youth's shoulder, and the pair headed back to the towering edifice they called home. Here, in the south of France, history was a living thing. Hundreds of years could crowd a given moment, and Jean-Pierre and his wife, Eleanor, had often speculated about the story that the manoir could tell, if only it could talk. For it had stood, as it did now, during the proud moment a century earlier, when the Navarrese Henri ascended the throne of France. Before that, it had weathered those turbulent times when Catholic and Protestant brethren turned on each other and shed each other's blood.

Of particular interest to Eleanor, it had stood earlier still, during those distant and hazy days of the twelfth century, when the southland had a mind of its own and men and women of the Cathar faith roamed freely, healing the sick and administering the *consolamentum*. The consolamentum was a vow that freed one from his or her wicked coil and put them on a path that led to the waiting arms of a true and loving God. The Catholic Church considered the Cathars to be heretics and went so far as to mount a crusade against them. As a result of this crusade, the Cathars were thought to have been wiped out, slaughtered like animals and burned like rubbish. But Jean-Pierre and his wife knew that a few had survived, persisting down through the centuries, and that Eleanor, herself, was one.

Now, with the implementation of the Dragonnades and the soldiers on their way, she was afraid that her secret would be discovered, and Jean-Pierre tried to be patient with her. In his mind, his status as a courtier would protect them both—him as a Protestant and her as the fellow Calvinist that others therefore assumed her to be. He scoffed at Eleanor's concerns that if the Catholic king considered Protestants such an affront that he tried to force their conversion by billeting dragoons in their homes, then how would he respond to finding a Cathar in his realm?

As they neared the manoir, Pierre left his father's side and hurried toward the barracks, where a couple of Jean-Pierre's bodyguards hunkered from the mistral in the shelter of one of the walls, playing cards. The men loved to let the boy pull up a stool when they played their games, sharing their lewd jokes and treating him as one of their own, and Jean-Pierre couldn't imagine that his son would not always enjoy such privilege, because this was the life he'd been born to. This was who he was destined to be.

Joining them, Jean-Pierre watched the two guardsmen play their hands. He couldn't resist pointing out to the one named Thierry that the mistral could steal his cards and show them to his opponent if he did not grip them tighter. Thierry and Arnaud both laughed, slapping the table and reshuffling, and Jean-Pierre and his son took their leave. Eleanor met them at the manoir door, her face etched with the worry that she carried of late. Pierre pecked her on the cheek and made for the stairs, while Jean-Pierre steered her toward the drawing room.

"Any news?" she queried.

"Everything will be okay," he assured her. "Tomorrow we will leave for Versailles and will be gone a fortnight at most. There is nothing to worry about."

"But what if it's too late? What if the king has made up his mind and it can't be changed? What will we do when his soldiers arrive and are at our door?"

Jean-Pierre shook his head.

"Do you not trust me?" he challenged her.

"Of course, but . . ."

"Do you not have faith that I can protect my family? My home?"

"Of course, my love," she demurred.

"There you have it, then!" he exclaimed, reveling in the sense of power that coursed through his veins. He could never have imagined that Eleanor had a valid point that was well worth considering, for in his mind, he was not the sort of man to whom things simply happened. He was the one who pointed and made his wishes known. He always had others to do his bidding, and they were eager to comply.

◆　◆　◆

By dawn the following morning, final preparations for Jean-Pierre's departure were well underway. The soldiers who served as his bodyguards rolled their bedrolls and swept the barracks floor. They fed their horses extra rations of oats and oiled their muskets. Inside the manoir, Eleanor laid out clean clothes on Jean-Pierre's bed. She insisted on doing this herself, with lingering touches on the leather breeches that were for traveling, and the wool jacket and waistcoat for his appearance in court.

Then, all too soon, there was no more reason for delay, and Jean-Pierre mounted his horse and made himself comfortable in the saddle. Eleanor stood at the manoir door, alongside Pierre. Jean-Pierre had considered taking the boy along, for he was already as tall as most men. That was the way of the du Lauxes, Jean-Pierre thought proudly. The family men ran tall and angular. There had been a day when they jousted in tournaments, and their bodies still bore vestiges of a readiness for battle.

In the end, however, he'd decided to leave his son where he would be a comfort to his mother. For if her concerns about the Dragonnades persisted, who better to confide in than the son who adored her? Who more suited to allay her silly fears, Jean-Pierre thought, as he turned his horse and took his place at the head of the waiting column.

Guy Aguirre, riding at his side, seemed relieved to finally be on the move. Guy was more than the captain of his seigneur's guard, he was Jean-Pierre's friend and erstwhile mentor in matters pertaining to the martial arts, and it was he who had taught Jean-Pierre how to wield a rapier.

"The Sun King is a fair man," Guy opined. "You have done more than any of the other nobles, supporting his causes and standing by him when he needed you. Surely, he will listen to whatever you have to say!"

"I have served the king very well," Jean-Pierre agreed, nodding.

"And loyally!" Guy said, with fervor. "Surely, the king knows the value of his courtiers and is fully aware that a man doesn't have to be a Catholic to assist in his deliberations!"

"*Exactement*," Jean-Pierre said.

He might have said more, for he had indeed served the Sun King loyally and brimmed with pride at the thought of it. But just then a singing voice rose from the rear of the column. There were eight men in all, wearing leather cuirasses and carrying muskets in the crooks of their arms. They had just spent nearly a month at the manoir, where they had fallen under the spell of their beautiful hostess, and one of them began to sing—not one of the drinking songs that travelers sang in the roadside auberges, when they were tired and surly, but the dulcet refrain of a lost love. Soon, the other men joined in, softy, sweetly for such rough men.

Guy shot his seigneur a grin, and Jean-Pierre softened. He knew the effect his wife had on other men. It was part of the magic with which she was so abundantly blessed. She had the gift of making others feel good when they were around her, and he allowed himself the indulgence of the fortunate man and proud husband he knew himself to be.

◆ ◆ ◆

As the sun reached its high point in the now cloudless sky, the group stopped to rest under the thin canopy of a stand of scraggly trees. Jean-Pierre retrieved a linen bundle from one of his saddlebags and the men gathered around, their eyes dancing at the sight of the meat pies his wife had prepared. The travelers knew full well that later in their journey, they would have to resort to hard cheese for their repasts, along with bread that would become increasingly difficult to chew. But for now, they had stewed venison wrapped in crispy pastry, and more than one tongue swiped at smacking lips.

"If my wife could cook like this, I'd be twice the man that I am," Thierry said, accepting his portion gratefully. Breaking the meat pie open, he raised it to his nose and inhaled the medley of spices— thyme and sage, fennel and, of course, lavender. His face softened and he closed his eyes as he took a bite.

"If your wife could cook like this, you might not have her for long," another of the men said, grinning in a manner that showed he meant no disrespect.

Jean-Pierre caught Guy looking at him in that careful, lidded way of his and wondered how much the man knew. There was no question that Guy loved Eleanor and would have given his life for her if called to the task. But unlike Jean-Pierre, Guy had never been burdened with the knowledge of Eleanor's particular faith. He had not had to make the choice of whether or not to allow someone, whom even Protestants would have viewed askance, into his heart and into his life.

Setting such thoughts aside for the moment, Jean-Pierre lowered himself to a grassy patch at the base of one of the trees and closed his eyes. He was not used to the saddle and travel fatigue stole over him. He dreamed of his wife on the day they'd first met, a tall, elegant woman with hair the color of sunset and eyes of the bluest sky. Eleanor's sister, Esclarmonde, was famed for her beauty, and Jean-Pierre had, in fact, gone to the family château to seek Esclarmonde out. But once he saw Eleanor, he could think of no one else, and in his sleep, his heart ached, the way it did so intensely in dreams. When he learned Esclarmonde had taken the consolamentum at the age of eighteen and that Eleanor planned to follow, he might well have abandoned any designs that he had toward her, for the vows of a parfaite required celibacy. But love's arrow had already struck, and Eleanor must have felt the bite as well. For while she had expressed every intention of following in her sister's footsteps, she waited until after the birth their son, Pierre, whom she and her husband agreed would be their one and only child.

◆　◆　◆

Jean-Pierre awakened to a light touch and saw Guy bending over him. Even in the shade, the heat had become insufferable, and Jean-Pierre had a headache. He felt disoriented and short-tempered. Not too far distant, a deer stood in the road, which only added to his discontent, as if the apparent trust it displayed was far too much of a burden to place on such a groggy and increasingly surly group of men.

The heat seemed to pull at his tongue as he mounted up. Sweat trickled down his neck. Flies looped and landed, crawled and irritated. Long trips were like this, he thought, wearily, trying to reason with himself. You had moments of vigor and moments when you didn't want to take another step.

They had not gone very far when Guy reined his mount to a stop.

"Something wrong, *mon ami?*" Jean-Pierre said, trying not to sound as disinterested as he felt, and Guy glanced at him sharply, before returning his attention to what lay ahead. The road had been mostly flat up to this point, but now it dipped down into a little swale, where a tangle of trees crowded a small stream of water. The road disappeared into the woods, where it followed a hidden course, before emerging once again and climbing the hill on the far side. A buzzard wheeled lazily overhead, too far away to make a shadow.

"Okay, what is it?" Jean-Pierre relented.

Guy frowned. Turning in his saddle, he nodded at Thierry and gestured toward the woods. Thierry gave him a blank look. Then his face hardened and he heeled his horse to a trot, skirting Guy and Jean-Pierre. Nearing the woods, he slowed to a walk, paused briefly, then entered the gloom.

"We've never had any trouble on this road," Jean-Pierre observed, irritably.

Guy looked at him with dark, brooding eyes.

"The hare only meets the hawk once," he grunted.

With some effort, Jean-Pierre held his peace. A man like Guy knew that a clump of trees sometimes held a secretive heart that thrived on moldering obscurity, and Jean-Pierre would normally have applauded such reasonable caution. But the man could be overly wary at times, he thought. Not every tree hid a brigand.

The thud of horse's hooves came from inside the woods and Thierry emerged into the sunlight. He pulled his mount to a stop in front of Guy and kept a tight rein, holding the spirited animal in place. "All clear," he said, as the horse danced to the left and then side-stepped to the right.

Guy motioned for the man to fall back into the column, but otherwise didn't budge, as if some sixth sense continued to warn him of a danger that he couldn't put his finger on. Jean-Pierre had finally had enough. Jostling his heels, he ordered the column forward, heading into the tunnel of trees, with packed earth that darkened and then began to soften where a small rivulet crossed the road. A myriad of prints tracked the mud. The cloven hooves of deer and feral hog, the tracks of the many birds that had come to drink. The wheel ruts and human footprints were old and rounded, yielding to the process of erosion that would smooth them to creases and dimples before eliminating them entirely. None of the human spore was fresh.

Guy caught up to his seigneur.

"Something's not right," he said.

Jean-Pierre turned to give a retort, but Guy had pulled up his horse and sat frozen in the saddle. For up ahead, where the road broke out of the woods into a blaze of sunlight, sat a rider. He wore a voluminous red robe and a red skullcap. A silver cross hung around his neck. He appeared to be alone, waiting.

"*Merde*," Jean-Pierre breathed.

He heeled his horse forward.

"Who are you and what do you want?" he demanded, with a look that would have withered most men. There was no doubt the stranger was a cardinal, which concerned him. For while he thought he knew everyone of any importance in the surrounding countryside, he had never met this man before. Also, cardinals rarely traveled without an entourage, which alerted him to the nagging possibility that all was not as it seemed.

Guy took his place at Jean-Pierre's side.

"Give the word, seigneur, and I will clear the way," he growled, shifting the reins to his left hand, and slipping his right to the grip of his musket.

"Just hold," Jean-Pierre said, dismissive of the easy solutions that soldiers seemed to favor, and wary of acting hastily toward an emissary of Rome.

"A wise choice," the cardinal said, coldly. He gave his head a small sideways twitch, and it was only then that Jean-Pierre noticed the other men, hidden in the trees alongside the road. They had dismounted and stood as shadows within the gloom, their muskets leveled. A chill ran through him.

"How dare you accost us? State your business!" he cried.

"I am Phillipe Neuve, in the service of Our Lord and Savior," the cardinal said.

Guy gasped. "The Spaniard!"

Jean-Pierre's skin crawled. Of course he had heard of the one they called the Spaniard, but he was supposed to be in Spain and not here. Surely the king had the Dragonnades to do his dirty work. He had no need to avail himself of the special talents of one of the Church's inquisitors.

"Let us pass," Jean-Pierre said, icily.

"I have no interest in your men." The cardinal's eyes lingered on Jean-Pierre. "They are free to go on their way while you and I have a word." Slowly, as if each movement were the result of careful thought, he reined his horse around and waited.

Guy shot out a restraining hand and hissed, "He is the devil in church cloth."

"I will sort this out," Jean-Pierre assured him.

"No—"

But Jean-Pierre had already caught up to the cardinal and followed him out of the woods, leaving Guy and the rest of the column behind. The cardinal rode up a small rise and stopped. His eyes drifted past Jean-Pierre to the distant horizon, and he remained serene during the sudden cascade of gunfire that erupted from the trees behind them. A haze of smoke rose through the spreading branches.

Paralyzed with utter disbelief, Jean-Pierre's mind raced, plunging from its pinnacle of superiority into an awaiting abyss. Wheeling his horse around, he charged back toward the woods. But one of the cardinal's men met him at the tree line and grabbed his horse's bridle. The animal shied and sidestepped. More men emerged from the woods, their faces grimly set. They escorted the struggling seigneur back to the waiting cardinal.

"What have you done?" Jean-Pierre cried.

The cardinal regarded him patiently.

Jean-Pierre twisted in the saddle. The trees looked so calmly composed now, their dark secret hidden. The blue sky and sprawling terrain seemed unaffected by what had just transpired.

"Come—we have a long way to go," the cardinal said, as if speaking the voice of reason to a child.

Jean-Pierre was taken to a villa a long and painful ride from the desolate woods where he'd been arrested. He was too stiff to dismount, and one of the cardinal's soldiers pulled him from the horse, which a man in a black monk's robe then led away. The cardinal, who had offered no explanations during the journey, now claimed to have pressing matters to attend to, and left Jean-Pierre in the care of a youthful but otherwise undistinguished person with the inquisitive but hesitant demeanor of a scholar.

"Please follow me, monsieur," the scholar said, deferentially.

"Who are you . . . and what kind of monster is he?" Jean-Pierre rasped, his gaze darting from the scholar to the departing cardinal. He shuddered and a wave of nausea swept over him.

The scholar gave him a pained look.

"I know you must have a lot of questions," he said. He raised his eyes as if the weight of the world were on his shoulders. It was the look of a man who put himself first and foremost, and who could only consider the suffering of another within the context of his own needs, whatever they might happen to be.

"I'm sure all will be made clear in due time," he suggested.

"In due time?" the seigneur gasped, his voice quavering. "Do you have any idea who I am? Do you have any idea what you've done?" he demanded, accusing the scholar of complicity in the misdeeds of his superior. "Do you know how much trouble you're in?"

The scholar glanced at one of the soldiers, and Jean-Pierre felt a firm hand against his back. He stiffened and twisted around to see who dared to treat him thus, and the hand gave a hard shove, propelling him forward.

The scholar led him to a small apartment that might have appeared almost comfortable except for the bars on the windows. It had a bed, bare walls, and a single upholstered chair. A chamber pot sat in one of the corners. "I hope you will not find your accommodations disagreeable," the scholar said, avoiding Jean-Pierre's distraught gaze. He hesitated, as if trying to decide what to say next. "I'm sure you and the señor will have much to talk about."

His mouth tugged with a hopeful, tentative smile.

"You surely don't expect me to stay here!" Jean-Pierre said.

The scholar's eyes widened. "Why, yes, I do. You will learn all you need to know about Señor Neuve soon enough. In the meantime, consider this . . ." The scholar raised a cautionary finger. "He is not a man to be trifled with. He will have many questions and you must take him seriously. I urge you to do everything he asks and give him what he wants—whatever that may be."

He paused again, and then his face brightened.

"I'm sure you wouldn't want to remain here any longer than necessary!"

His head bobbed as he turned toward the door.

"Wait!" Jean-Pierre said.

"You'll be perfectly fine," the scholar clucked, in his patronizing manner.

"Stop!" Jean-Pierre shouted.

But the scholar had already crossed the threshold, and the bolt thudded into place on the far side of the door. Jean-Pierre's heart beat frantically, as if coming alive in an otherwise dead body. He staggered to the door, pressing his hands against it, then lunged toward the barred window, hoping to catch sight of his interlocutor. But the courtyard outside blazed with the shimmering heat of a sunlit hell. Not even a sparrow stirred. Raising his hands to his face, Jean-Pierre tore at his forehead with his fingernails. Again, he heard the muskets in the far-off woods. Then, he thought of the manoir, with Eleanor and Pierre seeing him off from the open door, and a swoon of panic gripped him.

◆ ◆ ◆

JEAN-PIERRE PACED THE ROOM ON legs that threatened to buckle, if they bent at all. Wave after wave of incomprehension washed over him. Earlier in the day, his main concern had been the Dragonnades, and it made sense, up to a point, to think the cardinal was somehow connected to the king's obsession with the religious unification of his realm. But on closer examination, the argument didn't hold up. The pope certainly knew of the king's endeavors, and made no attempt to interfere, one way or the other. No, it was something else. The cardinal had nothing to do with the Dragonnades, Jean-Pierre was sure.

He continued to pace, positing one conjecture and then another, getting nowhere, as the now setting sun seemed to suck the light from the room. The whites turned to grays and then to charcoal. The room had no lamp, and he stood in the darkness, unwilling to undress or approach the bed. Then, when hours had passed and he finally sat down, the mattress felt cold and hard. A moon came up and shone through the window, and he wondered if it was the same moon that shone on the manoir. At some point, he lay back on the bed. He didn't try to sleep, but it must have happened, for he jerked awake and reached for his sleeping wife, only to suffer the abrupt realization that she was not there and that he was trapped in some unknown place, and that, for the moment at least, he was powerless to do anything about it.

The morning came with a flare of hope, and he awoke to a certainty that a terrible, horrible mistake had been made and that someone, anyone—maybe even his captor—would soon realize this. The Spaniard had a reputation for ruthlessness, but Jean-Pierre had no idea why he would be in the southland of France. The series of prosecutions now known as the Inquisition had originated in Albi, not far from Toulouse, to combat the Cathar threat to papal well-being. But that was hundreds of years ago. Even allowing that the current pope viewed Protestants in the same light that a previous one had viewed the Cathars, why would an inquisitor be here, where his jurisdiction was waning? Why had he singled out one Protestant nobleman among many? What did he want from someone like Jean-Pierre?

A sound came from the far side of the chamber door, and Jean-Pierre's heart leaped. He ran his fingers through his hair, brushed his face with his hands, and smoothed the wrinkles from his shirt. The door shuddered and squeaked open, and a monk in a black robe entered, carrying a tray that held a basket of bread and a pitcher of something to drink. A soldier loomed on the threshold of the portal behind him.

"Where is the man with the spectacles?" Jean-Pierre demanded, wishing he had learned the scholar's name.

The monk ignored him. Shuffling to one side of the door, he placed the tray on the tiled floor.

"I must speak to the cardinal at once!"

Without so much as a glance at him, the monk turned and left the room.

"Wait!" Jean-Pierre cried.

But now the soldier stepped fully inside and glared at Jean-Pierre until the seigneur relaxed his fists. Then, the soldier turned his back and strode after the monk, slamming the door behind him. Jean-Pierre seethed. The argument he had intended to make knotted up in him and his fury quickly leached into despair. His eyes traveled Heavenward, and he was unable to contain a moan. Picking up the tray, he flung it against the wall and then paced the floor like a lion in a cage, one minute determined to have the heads of everyone involved in his kidnapping and the next falling into a well of wretched desperation. For by now it was becoming clear to him that unless he could reason with his captors, no one else could help him. Assuming the king was not somehow involved in the abduction, even he could not intervene and save a man if he didn't know where he was.

◆　◆　◆

"Monsieur." The scholar poked his head into the room as if he were popping in on an old friend. Indeed, there had been a time when Jean-Pierre thought the scholar was sympathetic to him. But according to the scratches on the wall of the chamber, Jean-Pierre had been a prisoner for three weeks now, and but for their initial meeting, he hadn't seen the scholar in all that time. By now, the king would be well aware that one of his courtiers was missing and would have sent missives to the manoir. Jean-Pierre could only imagine that Eleanor was sick with worry.

"It's Señor Neuve," the scholar said, apologetically. "He wishes to speak with you, if it's not an inconvenience."

Jean-Pierre glared. By now, his hair had started to mat and an aggressive beard gripped his chin and throat. His clothes had taken on an alarming pungence.

"If it's not an *inconvenience*?" he asked in disbelief.

The scholar nodded. "Señor Neuve has his ways," he sighed. "He has this notion that if you give someone enough time to think about things, they will be much easier to talk to. He doesn't see the need for harsher methods." The scholar paused. "He is very enlightened, compared to some of the other inquisitors. You would readily concur, I assure you, if you only knew."

"Harsher methods?"

"Why yes." The scholar blinked. "You've no doubt heard of the rack and other instruments of . . . persuasion?"

"Harsher than murder?" Jean-Pierre said. "The cardinal murders my men and deprives me of my freedom, and you talk of harsher methods?"

The scholar gave a brief, chagrined nod, as if he had suspected all along that the seigneur might be difficult.

"Come," he said, in a decidedly weary tone. He took a step back and lifted a hand toward the open door, where a guard waited.

Jean-Pierre imagined wrapping his hands around the scholar's neck and squeezing until the life popped out of him. In the end, however, he followed after the man, because he had no other choice. His long-awaited interview was at hand, and he was agitated with no small fear as to what to expect. For as Jean-Pierre now surmised, the inquisitor either acted on behalf of the pope—albeit for reasons beyond Jean-Pierre's reckoning—which would have immunized him from accountability, or else the pope had no idea what his cardinal was up to, making the inquisitor a renegade, which was arguably much worse.

◆　◆　◆

THE INQUISITOR SAT AT A glass-topped desk in a chamber at the end of a long veranda. He no longer wore his red robe, but rather a white silk shirt, purple breeches, and felt slippers of the same color. Standing before his captor now after several weeks of anticipation, Jean-Pierre found himself trembling uncontrollably. He was not used to quailing in another man's presence and tried to get a rough grip on himself.

The cardinal set aside his quill and carefully blotted the parchment in front of him, moving with unhurried deliberation.

"Our good friend is enjoying his stay, I presume?" he said, directing his attention to his assistant, as if Jean-Pierre was not there.

"Your kindness has been a wonder, Your Eminence," the scholar assured him.

"You may address *me*, monsieur," Jean-Pierre said, purposefully using the mundane honorific instead of the more elevated one to which the cardinal was entitled. A flicker of annoyance crossed the inquisitor's face.

"As you wish," he said, his voice dry as scuttling leaves.

"What do you want from me?" Jean-Pierre demanded.

"A man who gets right to the point—I like that," the cardinal said, shooting a look of smug appraisal at his assistant. "It saves so much time in the end, and time is something we have so little of, wouldn't you say? You've had ample opportunity to think of this, I'm sure, and I applaud your directness."

"Just answer my question."

"Ah, so you're the inquisitor now, is that it?" the cardinal mused. The slight smile that twisted his lips was not at all comforting. "You've no doubt come to the conclusion that I have no business here. If we were in Rome, you would have no recourse but to face my interrogations. But the Church has slowed its pursuit of Protestants in the Languedoc and you are therefore safely beyond the reach of someone such as I. Is that what you're thinking?"

Leaning back in his chair, the cardinal knitted his fingers together in front of him. His eyes were like black stones.

"But that would be assuming that your apostasy is what concerns me—and frankly it does not, not at all," he continued. "Your king does not need the Inquisition to handle his religious affairs. He is doing quite well on his own, wouldn't you say? The Dragonnades were a stroke of genius. Who wouldn't rather convert to Catholicism than have a bunch of dirty, lecherous soldiers move into their homes and live with them? Granted, the expediency of such conversions is problematic . . . but that is not my concern—not for the moment, anyway.

"No, my friend, you Protestants are the least of my worries," the cardinal continued, with a dismissive wave. "Isn't it curious that we are only a crow's flight from where the Inquisition first started and was put to such good use?" His eyes narrowed as he watched for any reaction that Jean-Pierre might have. "There was a time when your Languedoc, as you call it, was so infested with heresy that the pope had no choice but to act. But we celebrated our victory too soon, didn't we? In our haste to move on and purify the faith elsewhere, we overlooked the possibility that the most poisonous weed of all still lingered, right here, where it had once proliferated. Right under your king's nose, if only he knew."

Jean-Pierre seethed. Although not a Cathar himself, he was married to one, and bristled at the hypocrisy of the cardinal's Church. The way he saw it, the Cathars' main sin was that they were so successful in the Languedoc, which was a fertile and wealthy land. The faith hailed from Mary Magdalene, as opposed to Saint

Peter, which caused the Church of Rome much umbrage. It elevated women as well as men, and many a noble family of the twelfth century—when the faith flourished—included Cathar mothers and daughters. More importantly to the Church, the wealth of such families went into coffers other than Rome's.

"You are the abomination!" Jean-Pierre spat. "Those so-called heretics posed a harm to no one. This was their land and you took it from them. The 'purification' you refer to was outright and villainous thievery!"

The cardinal shook his head with open disdain.

"Be that as it may, why would I concern myself with a mere Protestant, when an even bigger prize is at hand?" he said. "Don't look at me like that. I have heard that a Cathar still lives and that you harbor her." The cardinal raised a hand and clenched it into a fist, as if crushing the life from a baby bird. "You must tell me everything you know, and then—only then—perhaps God will have mercy on you and set you free."

The cardinal's eyes blazed with hatred, and with something else. There was a neediness. The desire to find something others had overlooked. The hunger of someone not satisfied with who he was, and who desired desperately to be much more.

Jean-Pierre was aghast. Three weeks in confinement had weakened him, and a sudden terror overwhelmed him—not for himself but for one he was now powerless to protect.

"My wife is no business of yours!" he cried.

The inquisitor slapped his hands down upon his desk in triumph.

"There it is," he said, beaming at his assistant.

Jean-Pierre's heart pounded. "What?"

But the cardinal no longer seemed interested in him. His chin sank to his chest. Perhaps it was the toll that victory sometimes takes, when the pressure of a consuming drive has suddenly lessened. There could be little doubt now that the Spaniard had acted alone, that he had taken great risks by incarcerating one of the southern French noblemen, and that the possible repercussions of his actions had weighed heavily.

"I have said nothing!" Jean-Pierre wailed, beseeching first the inquisitor and then turning his frantic gaze upon the scholar. But Jean-Pierre was alone in the horror of his betrayal. Neither the cardinal nor his assistant paid him any heed.

As if on cue, a black-robed monk entered the room. At a gesture from the cardinal, the monk slipped a hood over Jean-Pierre's head, and in the sudden darkness, with his own moist, hot breath smothering him, the seigneur panicked. The tread of booted feet approached and strong hands gripped his arms.

"Let me go!" he cried.

"Take our guest to his new accommodations," the cardinal said.

The words echoed in Jean-Pierre's head as he was dragged from the room. A flood of heat struck him, and he guessed they must have exited the villa. Then he smelled horses. He heard the squeak of a door and hands lifted him at the elbows, pitching him forward and onto a bench. He could smell the stink of another human body in close proximity.

Then, the bench lurched and he knew he was in a carriage. The hooves of the horses clipped and clopped as the carriage trundled along. Imagining that even now the cardinal was on his way to the manoir to seize his prey, Jean-Pierre tried to wrench off the hood. His arms, however, were pinioned. He tried to lurch to his feet but hit his head on the ceiling of the conveyance and was summarily yanked back down. The exertion and the suffocating hood proved to be too much, and he passed into oblivion.

Sometime later, he roused to find himself lying on his side. Thinking he must still be in the carriage, he kicked out a foot but found only empty air. The heat and moisture of his breath told him the hood was still on. But his hands were no longer tied, and he used them to push himself upright. He yanked the hood free, but the darkness remained unchanged. His hands fluttered to his forehead, his eyes. Then, panting, he reached out into the surrounding darkness, trying to get a sense of where he was. His hand fell on something that squirmed and squealed and bolted from his touch.

Shuddering, Jean-Pierre jerked back. The hairs on his neck stood up and his body spasmed. Once he found his courage again, he started crawling. His hands grew slick from the damp stone, and his knees grew wet and cold. He paused, reaching out an arm and waving it about, advancing and then pausing again. Soon, he felt the cold, hard surface of a stone wall. Then he crawled in the opposite direction until he found another wall. On his third blind jaunt, his hand encountered the damp, spongy surface of what he surmised to be the mat he had been lying on earlier. Shuddering, he backed away until he reached a wall, then pulled his knees up and gripped them tightly. He heard a groaning and thought someone was in the cell with him, only to realize that when he shut his mouth the sound stopped, and when he opened it, the sound started back up again.

◆　◆　◆

In endless darkness, he felt as if he drifted, like a winged creature hovering in the night. If he turned his chin to the left or to the right, it made no difference, for the darkness was the same. One time, he wandered from his mat on one of his exploratory missions and got lost. He knew the mat must have been near enough to touch but couldn't find it with his groping hands, and his heart pounded hard enough to burst. His breath came in pants, and he thought he would die of fright, before once again finding his pallet.

When his jailer slid trays of food through the slot at the bottom of the door, a sudden bar of light would leap out of the darkness. At first, Jean-Pierre was too slow. The scurrying of rats and mice, followed by sudden silence, let him know the bread was gone, and he had to console himself with the foul-smelling bowls of watered-down wine. The passage of time meant nothing in the darkness, and he had to wait with heightened senses for the distant sounds that indicated another feeding time was near, in order to beat the vermin to the tray and get any solid food at all.

Surely, he couldn't have survived very long under such circumstances.

"Someone is coming," the soft burr of a woman's voice warned, and he yelped.

"Who's there?" he rasped, straining to see.

There was no response, and he wrapped his arms around himself and huddled. Then he began to rock back and forth. When his legs tingled and finally went numb, he dropped down on his side and curled into a ball, fearing he was going insane. He thought of staggering to his feet, lowering his head, and charging against an unseen wall, seeking the arms of a merciful death.

"You must live," the voice said, and this time Jean-Pierre had enough courage to put a name to it.

"Eleanor?" he whispered, hoarsely.

"This is not how you will die," the voice said, but from a different direction this time, and he crawled off the straw pallet and lurched forward, his hand reaching.

"Eleanor?" he called out again, louder this time, fearful of his own voice, the sound it made, and what it might mean if no one answered. Then, he began to weep, for he knew he must be imagining things. He had crawled along the walls many times and found no one else in the cell with him. And he was certain that, even if she were there, the woman he had betrayed would have nothing more to do with him.

Squeezing his eyes shut, Jean-Pierre tried to address the one he blamed for his misery—a God who beckoned to all but who then set his children against each other and ignored them when they went to war. It shouldn't be that difficult, he reasoned. As a courtier, he had murmured in the Sun King's ear many a time and once you have spoken to one king, speaking to another should not be hard.

And at first, the words came. He pleaded and argued as if his God were there with him, as indeed he wanted so dearly to think that he was. But then the words seemed to get lost, and he could no longer find them. Jean-Pierre panted, the words like butterflies that had rested on his lips and then fluttered away. The emptiness inside of him echoed the emptiness of his cell, and he didn't know if he still lived or had been dead a long time now.

"Someone's coming," the voice said again, more insistently this time, and a sudden clamor filled the cell. The door squealed on its hinges, and a man entered, holding a lantern, the darkness fleeing around him like flights of crows.

Jean-Pierre raised up on an elbow and shielded his face with an arm. The tall forehead and bespectacled eyes, the mouth that puckered and opened before saying anything. It was the scholar. Jean-Pierre looked at him in awe, wondering if he were real or only another of the phantoms that had plagued him.

"Oh my," the scholar said, holding the lantern aloft and looking around the cell. He sighed with obvious relief. "Thank God you're not dead. Señor Neuve forbade me to visit and I thought . . . I was afraid . . ."

His face glistened wetly in the lamplight.

"My wife," Jean-Pierre croaked, through lips that were blistered and cracked.

"Your wife? Oh!" the scholar said. His face went through a slow transformation, as if he had entered the cell with one thought but now awakened to another. He blinked, owlishly.

"Yes, of course—your wife . . ." he said.

"Is she well? Has the inquisitor harmed her in any way?"

"Well, no," the scholar mused. "I mean, she is quite well indeed. There are many things in life to fear, but Señor Neuve is no longer one of them. He is . . . well, let's just say he is no longer an impediment to your happiness."

The scholar hesitated, before pressing on. It seemed important to him to make something very clear.

"It was his idea to put you here in the first place and not mine," he pointed out. "It was the way he worked, you see. He thought that with more time, you would be easier to talk to, in case there was anything more that he wanted to know. And then there was your wife to consider, and yes, you had every right to be concerned at the time. Señor Neuve was sure that with you here and under his control, she was bound to be more agreeable." The scholar paused. "You have to realize how much he wanted her. He would not have rested until she revealed to him every detail of her wicked heresy, and then, once she had completely and utterly confessed, he would have taken her to Rome in chains and put her on display for all to see."

"But why?" Jean-Pierre gasped, anguished at the scholar's words. "My wife has harmed no one. What has she done to deserve such insult?"

"Well, it's the *idea*—don't you see? An idea is a powerful thing—powerful enough to launch ships and set armies in motion. If I may beg our Lord's pardon, Christianity itself is just an idea, and imagine if people got to thinking there was a truer faith, as the Cathars believed. Imagine the damage it could cause, if it were allowed to go unchecked. No." He shook his head. "On this point Señor Neuve was right and I absolutely agree with him.

"But that is no longer your concern," he went on. "He will no longer be a trouble to you, I promise. Your wife is perfectly safe . . . for now."

"I don't understand . . ."

But the scholar seemed to have made up his mind about something. A glow kindled in his secretive eyes, and his haughty regard assumed a predatory glint.

"I must go, but rest assured I will return soon," he said, backing hurriedly toward the door.

"Take me with you!" Jean-Pierre shouted, lurching up from his pallet.

But the scholar showed no inclination to heed him. The look he gave the seigneur seemed to measure the man and come up with a very private assessment. Something was afoot, something that had nothing to do with Jean-Pierre's best interests, and as the scholar left the cell, carrying the lantern with him, the darkness flooded back in a most malevolent way.

◆ ◆ ◆

LANTERN LIGHT ONCE AGAIN FLOODED the cell as the scholar returned, this time with other men in tow. They brought a bed frame and a mattress, a writing table and a chair. They swept the floor with a broom, washed it down with buckets of water, and then swept it again. Meanwhile, the scholar produced writing quills, ink, and a blotter. He surveyed the room, then nodded with satisfaction.

Jean-Pierre stared at him, questions racing through his mind.

"Are we going to see the cardinal now?" he rasped, hesitantly.

A flicker of annoyance crossed the scholar's face.

"I thought we discussed this already?" he said. "Forget about the cardinal—it will be just you and me from now on. And things will be much better, like I promised."

"You will let me go?"

The scholar's gaze shifted away, and Jean-Pierre felt the heaviness of a dread that regardless of what may have happened to the inquisitor, nothing much had changed for the prisoner.

"I will do my best to secure your release," the scholar assured him. "In the meantime, I can only imagine how much you miss your family—and they you. Madame du Laux, for one, must be in despair! *Now* . . ." He waved at the writing materials on the table, "you can correspond with her and let her know you are well. You can let her know you are thinking of her and looking forward to returning to her soon. You can write as often as you like—every day if it pleases you—and I will make sure your letters are delivered."

He placed the lantern on the desk. His face hovered in the glow like a fearful orb.

"The next time I come, I will bring a proper reading lamp," he said, glancing down at the lantern, critically. "For now, we will have to make do with what we have. It is a harsh light, I grant you, but it is surely better than nothing!"

With that, he turned and left the cell, and Jean-Pierre now gazed about him in wonder. After so long in the darkness, in which days had turned into weeks, and weeks into God only knew what,

the visual details were like a rough-and-tumble assemblage of unexpected and shocking things. A bed with a mattress. A table and
chair. A floor now covered with carpets. The lantern spread its halo
of light, and a prayer of thanksgiving bubbled into his throat.

◆　◆　◆

WITH HIS NEW AMENITIES, JEAN-PIERRE found a measure
of comfort, inasmuch as warmth and dryness made a difference.
He started pacing back and forth from one wall to the next in an
attempt to keep his legs limber. He would squat down, as if to pick
something up off the floor, then straighten back up again. He lay
on his belly and pushed himself up with his arms until they shook
and burned. The scholar came to visit every day, bringing bread and
cheeses, sometimes even a pastry filled with berry jam, and time
passed in its fashion.

The scholar appeared to be sympathetic, fussing at him like a
thoughtful companion, and indeed, the two men did form a bond,
of sorts. The scholar always came with a guard, and when Jean-
Pierre demanded to be released, the bespectacled man shook his
head in the regretful manner of one who had very little control
over things. Eventually, the seigneur's demands softened. His voice
became a whisper. The scholar's eyes would drift toward the blank
pages lying on the writing table, as if to point out that the seigneur
was not without resources, and Jean-Pierre took the rebuke to heart.
Truly, the one thing that kept him alive was the love he bore for his
wife and son, and the happiness that even a dream can provide for
one humbled by such blighted confinement.

Then, finally, he sat down. Brushing his hand against a blank
page, he moistened his lips and glanced at the quill, which was

about ten inches long and with the feathers removed. Opening the bottle of ink, he gave it a sniff before setting it down. A dreaminess came over him. Taking a deep breath, he inked the quill. When he touched the paper and moved his hand, a dark line formed. Entranced, he watched the words that began to flow.

My dearest, darling sweetheart . . . he wrote.

FOUR

———————●———————

Many years later, a *commis de police* in the commune of Toulouse looked down at the complaints on the desk in front of him. He thought he would start with the *boulanger*, as the second complaint was from a local priest, and churchmen made him weary.

"Have you talked to this . . . baker?" the commis asked.

At a nearby desk, his assistant, Gaspar, shook his head.

"I thought you'd take particular interest in such a visit. I've heard they have delightful pastries."

"Ah, you should've told me right away—a *pastry* thief!" the commis said, feigning outrage, at which Gaspar snorted and grinned. The commis's love of confections was well-known.

Gaspar went on to explain that the baker had a special customer for whom he had made bread every day for a very long time. The customer's name was Geoffroi Gaston and he picked up the bread in person and carried it away with him. He always paid with money out of his pocket.

"A good customer," the commis said, nodding.

Gaspar glanced at him sharply, as if unsure whether or not his superior was being serious or making fun.

"One could call him that, indeed. But then something changed. Gaston complained that the modest allowance he received had run out, and he asked for credit. The baker was reluctant to agree, as he had his own bills to pay, but Gaston had been a good customer, as you've already observed. So the baker agreed, and Gaston started paying him when he could, sometimes after a week had gone by and then, more and more often, after a month or more. Then, there came a point when Gaston could not pay at all."

The commis listened intently.

"So this Gaston owed the baker money that he could not pay?"

Gaspar nodded, raising his hands and letting them drop again.

"Well then, we better not waste any more time," the commis said, rising from his desk with an officiousness that belied his lack of enthusiasm. The bakery wasn't far and they could have walked. But the commis liked riding in the carriage. It gave him time to think, he liked to say.

The baker did not have anything to add that they didn't already know, so they only stayed long enough to find out where this negligent debtor, Gaston, lived. Leaving the shop, the commis couldn't help but cast a lingering eye on the brioche, choux, and macarons on display. But his wife had been reminding him lately that he wasn't as young as he used to be, and so he licked his empty lips and decided to return another day, when he could claim a special occasion.

Gaspar glanced at him as if discerning his thoughts. "Do you ever wonder where we'll be in ten years?" he asked, as the carriage trundled along.

"I try to avoid such depressing thoughts," the commis groused, putting an end to such speculation.

Before too long, they entered the neighborhood described by the baker.

"Well, here we are," Gaspar said, peering out of the carriage window.

"*Ce que tu dis,*" grunted the commis, pulling the latch and throwing his weight against the carriage door.

Before them stood a neat little cottage. The flowers in the boxes under the front window had wilted and were starting to brown. But there was nothing to suggest this home was very different from the others in the neighborhood. There was no placard that read Here Lives a Cheat or any other such thing. In fact, the commis had the fleeting thought that this was a case most likely based on misunderstanding. He dared to think he might be home for the noon meal and maybe he could even take what the people in the sundrenched south called a *siesta.*

Gaspar tried the door and found it unlocked. No surprise there, the commis thought. Unless you had something in particular to protect, what was the point of inconveniencing yourself when you wanted to do something as routine as entering your home? So far, nothing appeared to be out of the ordinary. The commis was thinking that he hadn't made love to his wife in over a fortnight, and that if he resolved this complaint quickly, he might surprise her.

Inside the house, though, things started to get interesting. In the kitchen, they found a table set for one, with a plate and a single spoon. A clean, empty wine glass sat on the table, within easy reach of the one and only chair. A piece of folded paper made a neat tent atop the plate.

"We might as well take a look around," the commis said, shying away from the tented paper for the moment. The house had a profound stillness, and for some reason, the hairs on his neck stood up. Cupping his hand against the back of his head, he ran it down his neck as he went to a bookshelf full of bound volumes.

Literacy was rare at a time when most people couldn't write their names, and with his educational background, which included a year in the seminary, the commis took an interest in the reading material of other educated persons. The bookshelf held treatises by Abelard, Montaigne, and Descartes, which wasn't all that remarkable for a learned man.

But the other books gave the commis pause. Books by authors such as Jacques-Auguste de Thou, Pierre d'Avity, Jean Bodin, and more of the same ilk. Such authors would have meant nothing to a casual observer. Even Gaspar might have overlooked them. But the commis had studied the Protestant Reformation at seminary. He knew that some of the French Calvinists had gone to great lengths to be viewed not as an offshoot of the Catholic Church, but as something separate, with a unique provenance that went back to Christ and his apostles. They claimed it was no coincidence that the geographical footprint of their faith matched that of such groups as the Waldensians and Cathars, and that, in fact, some of the earlier Christianities were iterations of a truer, uncorrupted faith.

The flaw in this alleged pedigree was that, in the past, the supposed connections between Calvinism and earlier Christianities had been based on biased, self-interested research. Now one tended to take a more objective look at firsthand sources, such as interviews with those considered to be heretics and notes from interrogations by the Dominican Inquisition. An idea took shape and began to develop in the commis's mind.

"Sir, look!" Gaspar said, standing in front of a desk on the opposite side of the room.

On the desk was a stack of paper that turned out to be an unfinished thesis. Glancing at the first page, the commis saw the word "Albigensian," which had been crossed out and the word "Cathar" written next to it. He caught his breath. He didn't know how the thesis related to unpaid bills at the bakery, but he couldn't shake the hunch that there was a connection.

"And here!" Gaspar said, holding open the lid of a storage chest along the wall. The commis hastened over and found a cache of letters, the folds smoothed out, gathered together by year and neatly tied with twine. Each bundle was thick as a book and there appeared to be dozens of them.

"What can this mean?" Gaspar wondered out loud.

The commis shook his head, at a loss for words. He decided it was time to take a look at the tented piece of paper on the plate in the kitchen. Picking it up, he glanced at it, casually at first and then more intently. It was a map and nothing more. No explanation of any sort.

"Commis!" Gaspar shouted.

He had continued his search of the house and now stood in front of the pantry, which normally would have held such items as baskets of garden vegetables and crocks of pâté. Indeed, such things were there. But there was something else, too. A man hung from the end of a rope, his belly bulging, his contorted, blackened face at an angle. He had neglected to take off his spectacles and they still pinched his nose.

"Sir, there's a note," Gaspar said, stepping back uneasily and pointing to a piece of paper pinned to the suspended man's shirt. He gave the commis a queasy glance before moving closer and squinting, trying not to touch the note as he read. "It says . . . to tell Seigneur Jean-Pierre du Laux that he's sorry. It says that he—the hanged man, that is—meant no harm. He begs the forgiveness of a merciful God."

Gaspar glanced at his superior, searching his face.

"It's . . . Gaston," he said, hoarsely.

The map still dangled from the commis's hand. He didn't know what it referenced but needed no further convincing that it was important. The complaint against a man who hadn't paid his bakery bill had suddenly blown up, turning into something that both excited the commis and teased with a hint of horror.

"Shall we cut him down?" Gaspar asked.

"We've got people who can take care of that," the commis said, unable to account for the revulsion that rose into his throat.

"But, sir," Gaspar said, dubiously. Already a faint stench had started to gather in the room.

"Leave him," the commis snapped, and turned and headed for the door.

◆　◆　◆

THE MAP WAS REALLY VERY good. The lines were well-composed, with neat, concise markings. Gaston had placed an "X" along a road the commis recognized as the Place d'Église, and before long, they found themselves in front of one of the commonplace stone-and-mortar farmhouses that dotted the outskirts of Toulouse. The roof had bald spots where tiles were missing, and most of the windows were broken. Seen from the road, it looked thoroughly abandoned.

The commis glanced at Gaspar.

"Do you think we should go in?" Gaspar asked, unenthusiastically.

In response, the commis thrust open the carriage door and got out. Glancing up at the driver, he bade him wait, then approached the house cautiously. The commis knocked, and when no one answered, he tried the door, which opened without resistance. Inside was a fireplace, with charred pieces of wooden furniture. Cobwebs were strung from the ceiling, and the floor was littered with dead flies and mouse droppings. Two doors led from the main room of the house, one of which opened to a stairway that rose to the second level. The other door was secured with a padlock.

"Why would the front door be open but then have a padlock here?" Gaspar wondered.

"I don't know, but I don't like it," the commis grunted.

He gestured toward the door with his head.

"Do you want me to force it?" Gaspar asked, nervously.

"We didn't come this far to turn back now."

Gaspar glanced around for some kind of tool. Finding none, he went outside and returned a few minutes later with a mallet.

"The carriage driver had this in his box," he explained. He struck the mallet against the lock. But the mallet was made of wood and the lock held. Gaspar gave his superior a glance and the commis nodded impatiently. Gaspar left once again and returned with a spanner wrench.

"I probably should have brought this the first time," he said.

He struck the lock repeatedly with the wrench until the hasp loosened. Then, after a few more blows, Gaspar was able to pull the door open and a damp, moldy breath of air rose from the darkness of the cellar below. Once more, Gaspar dashed from the house, this time returning with the running lantern from the carriage. He struck a flint to light the wick and held the lantern through the open cellar door.

Preceded by the glow of the lantern, they went down the wooden steps and found two bolted doors. No longer in need of the commis's goading, Gaspar removed the bolt from the first door and pulled it open. A foul odor spilled from the room, and Gaspar turned aside, covering his nose. Holding the lantern out in front of him, he peered into the room and then moved out of the way so the commis could see.

In front of them lay a room filled with desiccated human filth. A skeleton slumped in the corner, with one knee up and the other leg flung out as if the body had been arrested in the midst of a disjointed and ineffective burst of dying energy. The two policemen looked at each other.

"Could this be the Seigneur du Laux from Gaston's note?" Gaspar asked, and the commis didn't respond. His mind raced. How would an *academian* like Gaston know of a prison that no one else knew about? Whose skeleton was it and why was it here? If it was the seigneur Gaston referenced in his note, why tender an apology now, when it was clearly too late?

"Let's see the second room," the commis said, eager to leave this particular chamber and not at all sure he wanted a repeat experience in the next one.

But even before Gaspar got the second door open, the commis sensed that something was different. A sliver of light showed as the door cracked, then the glow of a lamplit chamber. There was a bed and an empty bookcase. At a writing table sat an old man with wiry gray hair that reached to his shoulders and a white beard that fell halfway down his chest. He had a broad brow and deep-set eyes that stared in wild alarm at the intruders. The man's face was as pale as the paper he had been writing on, and again, the eyes—the commis was sure he would never forget them for the rest of his life. They were the crazed eyes of someone who had been locked away in a cage and abandoned, while the world he once knew went on without him. The commis was not a man given to swearing, because he considered it the habit of a weak and undisciplined mind, but the only word he could think of was one that would have scalded the ears of his instructors at the seminary he had once attended.

◆　◆　◆

THE PRISONER, WHOM THE COMMIS now presumed to be the Seigneur du Laux from Gaston's note, could not seem to fathom what was happening. With the commis on one elbow and Gaspar on the other, he balked at the threshold of the chamber, his face writ with distress. Then, when they finally got him to the wooden steps, he peered upward like a frightened marmot from the depths of his hole.

"Are we going to see the Spaniard?" he asked.

Gaspar gave a questioning glance, and the commis shrugged.

"Do you want to see the Spaniard?" the commis asked.

The seigneur thought about it for a moment, then shook his head.

"No," he said, turning around as if to head back into his cell.

"Oh, come on," Gaspar huffed.

Though weakened by malnutrition and advancing age, the seigneur was still a tall man. Surely not as big as he had once been, the commis thought, but large enough that the two policemen had to half-drag, half-carry him up the steps and out into the daylight, where the prisoner recoiled, crying out and shielding his face from the sun.

When they reached the waiting carriage, he thrust out his arms, bracing himself on either side of the door, as if he feared to enter. Yielding to the pressure from Gaspar, he finally got in and sat down, patting his fingers against his face as if searching for something that wasn't there.

When they arrived at the police office, getting the seigneur out of the carriage was as difficult as getting him into it had been. He just sat there with his eyes closed, as if cutting himself off from the world would make it disappear, and no amount of coaxing would have him budge. On a hunch, the commis mentioned the word "Spaniard," and it had a surprising effect. The seigneur roused in a state of rage and stumbled from the carriage on his own, only to once again stand blinking and bewildered in the sunlight.

◆　◆　◆

Turning the seigneur over to Gaspar, the commis got back into the carriage to follow up on the other complaint he had received that morning—the one from the priest. But it was hard to get the seigneur out of his mind, and he pulled from his satchel a packet of letters he had taken from Gaston's house. While he was hesitant to advance a theory just yet, one thing was becoming clear. Someone had written thousands of letters over the course of what had to have been many years, and not one of them had been delivered.

The carriage pulled to a stop, and the commis kept reading. Then, he finally looked up to see a sprawling mansion and a man in a silk dressing gown and silk slippers standing in the open door, his hands on his hips, scowling. The commis sighed.

"It took you long enough to get here," the priest snapped.

"Begging your pardon," the commis said, using the voice he reserved for important, though difficult, people. The priest seemed mollified—for the moment, at least. He gave the policeman a cursory tour of the house, waving a fleshy hand at the elegant drapes and expensive tapestries. There were gilded pieces of art and Oriental carpets. On a table of oiled walnut stood a Chinese porcelain vase containing a large bouquet of silk flowers.

"Are you paying attention to me?" the priest demanded, noticing the commis's wandering gaze.

"Yes, of course," the commis countered, his eyebrows twitching. "You were saying?"

"What I am saying is that they were right there!" the priest sputtered, pointing toward the walnut table. "The *candlesticks. My* candlesticks, monsieur," the priest exclaimed, his eyes owlish as they searched those of the commis, looking for understanding and sympathy, any sign at all that the commis shared his outrage. "They were pure silver, a matched set, worth more than—"

The commis was sure the rest of the sentence had something to do with the pension that a policeman might expect. "Was anything else taken?" he coolly interrupted, looking around. "I can't help but notice that you are a man of discriminating taste, and it makes me wonder. Why would someone steal a pair of candlesticks and leave the rest?"

The priest's eyes narrowed.

"What are you suggesting?"

"I beg your pardon?"

"You think being a man of God is easy? I enjoy my collections, yes, but I have earned them. They are the blessings of a grateful God. To you, candlesticks may be nothing. But to me they are a sign of God's grace, along with everything else he has bestowed upon me. How the devil would I know how a criminal mind works? How would I know why a thief might choose a pair of candlesticks over something else? Your job is to find them and return them to me, not question my accounting of events."

The commis was more than a little taken aback by this outburst.

"I'm sorry you have gotten that impression," he replied, and would have said more to placate the irate man, but something caught his attention. Under a lacquered sideboard, almost hidden from view, was a black brocaded slipper too small to belong to the priest. It was a child's slipper, and the commis couldn't help but wonder what it was doing in the house of a churchman.

The priest followed his gaze, and a flush crept up the cleric's neck. He shifted his weight and then moved, so that his foot blocked the commis's view of the slipper. The commis recalled one of his teachers at the seminary telling him that being a priest was like walking a tightrope. At the time, he had thought the reference had something to do with the differences between good and evil and the two worlds a man of God might find himself in. Now, he wasn't so sure that the comment didn't mean that a person who walked a tightrope could topple to either side without warning.

The priest went on to describe how it felt to be robbed of something he treasured, the trespass and violation, the emptiness of the spot where the candlesticks had once stood, and the commis tried to pay attention. But more and more he thought of the case of the seigneur and the Spaniard, and he couldn't wait to get back to the police headquarters. Something was very definitely not right and the commis needed to know what it was.

◆　◆　◆

BY THE TIME HE GOT back to his office, the commis had read several more of the letters from Gaston's house, and an awful ache had grown in his chest. The letters contained the most tender endearments, and the outpouring of love was heartbreaking. But something else was in the words, too—remorse for something the correspondent never quite identified. In each subsequent missive, the remorse grew. The writer lamented that the one he called Eleanor had not responded to anything he had written, and far from blaming her, he seemed convinced this was entirely his fault.

Bursting into the room, the commis found Gaspar at his desk.

"Where is the seigneur?" he demanded.

"He's in the infirmary," Gaspar replied. "They have cleaned him up and trimmed his hair and beard. He looks almost normal again, with a new set of clothes. But wait. I checked in the archives, and there really is a Seigneur Jean-Pierre du Laux—or *was*, I should say. The man disappeared. And there's more . . ."

Gaspar's eyes danced. He leaned forward in his chair.

"I didn't think much of the name 'the Spaniard,' at first. After all, this close to the Pyrenees, that could have been just about anyone. But I did some more digging, and guess what? There was a particular person called the Spaniard who died just about the same time the seigneur disappeared. His name was Philippe Neuve and he was one of the inquisitors from Catalonia."

"An inquisitor!" The commis's head spun, for now he recalled learning of the renegade inquisitor who'd been convinced that Cathars still existed and had crossed into southern France in search of them.

"Neuve would have reported to Rome, but there is no record that he ever made an arrest. Apparently, Seigneur du Laux was a courtier and the king, himself, inquired after him. But neither hide nor hair of him was ever found. As far as anyone knew, Seigneur du Laux simply disappeared into thin air."

"So, you think this inquisitor might have detained the seigneur—illegally—and then died while the seigneur was in custody?" the commis said, trying hard not to show his own excitement. The disappearance of the two men at the same time seemed too much of a coincidence.

"That would explain a lot, wouldn't it?"

The commis paced in front of Gaspar's desk. "And then there's the puzzle of the two prisoners," he mused, stroking his chin.

"The two prisoners, sir?"

"There were two cells in the house where we found the seigneur," the commis said. "The first contained a skeleton. The cell was abominable, the man obviously uncared for. The cell with our seigneur in it, on the other hand, was fitted out like a cottage. There was a bed and a writing table, a lamp and writing materials—enough to let a man live in rudimentary comfort, as prisons go, anyway. And the question I have is *why*? Why was one man allowed to die in filth and the other kept alive?"

"Maybe the seigneur had something that Neuve wanted," Gaspar offered.

"But if our theory is right, Neuve was dead, remember? He might have put the seigneur in prison, but keeping him there was someone else's decision."

"You mean Gaston? What are you suggesting, that the one prisoner died and Gaston couldn't let the other one go, for fear of paying for the inquisitor's crimes?"

"Perhaps . . ." the commis said. "If Gaston was the one who didn't release the seigneur when the opportunity presented itself, and then the seigneur gained his freedom at a later point in time, Gaston would have had to explain himself. The seigneur was an important man who could have made things very difficult for him. The seigneur was aristocracy, for God's sake! But there's a piece missing . . . something that still doesn't add up. There's still the question of *why*. Why would a man like Gaston take such a big risk?"

"Maybe we should ask ourselves who Gaston was," Gaspar said, trying to be helpful and follow the commis's line of reasoning. "We know he was connected to the inquisitor in some way, but how? If he was really an academian—"

"Yes!" The commis snapped his fingers excitedly.

His thoughts raced to the letters, which the commis now knew had been written by the seigneur. He remembered the thesis that Gaston had been working on, and an idea that had teased at him now flowered. Certainly, an inquisitor who discovered the continuing presence of Cathars would have relished the opportunity to interrogate one of them—because that was what inquisitors did—and an unfortunate soul who was subjected to such questioning would have revealed what she thought her captor wanted to hear. An academian such as Gaston, however, might have realized that what an inquisitor wanted to hear reflected how much—or how little—he already knew, and fall short of a more meaningful truth. Gaston might have been interested in Cathars, too. But faced with the lingering mystery of who they really were—in their hearts and in their homes—and the opportunity to gain the trust of a man who was actually married to one, he might well have taken a different approach.

The commis rubbed a forefinger feverishly against his brow.

"Sir?" Gaspar said, frowning.

The commis had no time to explain.

"I must see the seigneur. Now!"

Gaspar lurched to his feet, but the commis had already bolted past him and through the adjoining door that led to what they called the infirmary. The room was small, with a bed and a chair, and a wooden table with bottles atop it. The windows let in a stream of light.

The street door of the infirmary opened, and a woman stepped in, carrying an armload of laundered towels.

"Where is he?" the commis demanded.

The woman stopped short.

"Where is who? The seigneur?" She glanced from left to right. "Why, he was right here!"

"Is something the matter?" asked Gaspar, who had followed on the heels of the commis.

"The seigneur is gone."

"Gone?" Gaspar said, glancing around much as the woman had done.

"I want him found!" the commis barked.

"He can't have gotten far, not someone in his condition," Gaspar offered.

But the commis was in no mood for idle speculation.

"I want him found and I want it done now! I don't care if you have to go to the ends of the earth!" he howled.

For he was convinced that he knew the truth at last. Discovering that a Protestant nobleman was married to a Cathar, a rogue inquisitor might have been willing to imprison the seigneur as a means of apprehending the follower of a religion that had once shaken the Church to its core. But after Neuve's death, Gaston was the one who kept the seigneur imprisoned, and for purely academic reasons. Gaston would have considered the seigneur's letters as a treasure trove of information. He couldn't deliver the letters to their intended without exposing the seigneur's illegal incarceration. But a lot could be learned from the sheer volume of the correspondence, and Gaston was willing to deprive a man of his freedom for no better reason than as research for a thesis.

The commis's head spun. Southern France had always been a complicated place. It could surprise and delight. It could take one's breath away. As a Catholic, the commis couldn't have cared less what God another person believed in or how they had come by their faith. As a policeman, however, he was driven to know the truth.

———•———

During Jean-Pierre's long incarceration, life had continued apace, and in far-off Penn's Woods, a granddaughter he knew nothing about knelt next to her bed, clasped her hands, and implored God to explain why life had to be so hard. Magdalena was only seven at the time. It had been less than a year since the fire that killed her sister and her sister's little baby, and she begged God to give her a reason why such tragedy had to happen.

With no response forthcoming, she finally got to her feet, dragging a heavy heart with her. Dressing dutifully, she paused at the window and watched as the sun seemed to cast first one leg and then the other over the heavily forested ridge to the east. First it skipped, then it hopped, and finally lifted in flight, and she shuffled in stockinged feet to the door and down the hall to the creaking stairs that seemed to her like a tunnel that burrowed into the earth.

Her mother stood at the stove, frying bacon in an iron skillet. That was the way it was in the mornings, the food preparation for a large family, frying the bacon and then the eggs, the toasting of yesterday's bread. There were six place settings at the table, along with a pitcher of milk and lumps of butter.

Magdalena's gaze drifted to the seventh spot, the now empty chair where Catharine had once sat. Magdalena had not spoken since the murders of her sister and her sister's baby, at the hands of the château's caretaker. Words seemed to wither and die on her tongue, ever since that moment when the wagon that she and her mother had ridden in crested the hill above the smoldering ruins, and even now, Magdalena could see them plain as day, the intertwined spirits of mother and child that had risen up in the column of bitter smoke. Even now, she saw the heavens open to receive the two souls and heard the rumbling growls of an earth that did not wish to give them up.

"Come on now and get to the table," Beatrice said, in her officious manner, for a mother of four surviving children on a pioneer farm did not have much time to dwell on the past. She raised her voice. "Jean? Andrew? Georgie? Come on, now, boys, while the breakfast is hot!"

There were three boys in all. They used to come tumbling down the stairs like puppies, tripping and falling over each other in their haste to be first at the table. But that was before. That was when things were different.

"I worry about you, child," Beatrice said, as the rest of the family scraped forks and knives against their plates. "How are you going to grow if you don't eat?"

Magdalena looked down at the small pile of food in front of her. Her mother didn't seem to understand how eggs soured in her throat and that the very thought of bacon made her gag.

"At least take a nibble. And another thing. It's about time you started talking to us again. It's not natural to stay bottled up the way you are. If you don't talk, you might forget how and think of the pickle you'll be in then!"

Magdalena's father, Pierre, cleared his throat and slid his chair back a little. He had finished his breakfast, along with the strong India tea, with cream and lots of sugar, that he'd ladled into his cup by the teaspoonful.

"Come here, *ma petite chou*," he said to Magdalena, patting a knee with a big hand. He smiled in that slow, careful way of his. "Come here and let me hold you. I haven't told you a story in a long time. Would you like to hear one?"

Tears darted to Magdalena's eyes as she climbed up onto her father's knee. She tilted her head against his shoulder. The warm arm that circled her waist reminded her of better times.

"Have I ever told you the story of how the wolf got its howl?" he asked, and she shook her head. "No? Well, it's a special one."

He paused long enough to make sure he had her rapt attention.

"You see, once upon a time, before wolves knew how to howl, there was a very special puppy, who was a lot like you. She saw how unfair life was—how one creature ate another and how so very few seemed to get along. Her brothers and sisters might have seen these things, too, had they bothered to look. But they were too busy, chasing grasshoppers and arguing among themselves."

He gave her a lingering look.

"Are you sure you want to hear this?" he teased, and she nodded eagerly.

"Well ..." Pierre said, then went on to say that since words got stuck in the poor wolf puppy's throat, she had no way to tell anyone about the sadness that she felt, until one day, she was so desperate that she bade her family farewell. They didn't want her to leave, of course. In fact, they begged her to stay! But she was determined to find her voice, and nothing they said could deter her. Alas, when she went to the north, her voice was nowhere to be found. She went to the south and then to the east and the west, but it wasn't there, either.

"But we are never as alone as we think," Pierre said, touching his finger to little Magdalena's nose. "The spirit of the mountains took pity on her. Our precious puppy had been unable to find her voice anywhere else, so the spirit of the mountains sent the wind to lead her in the only direction that was left." He lifted a finger, pointing upward. "The wind took her higher and higher, until at last she sat on a mountaintop, where the trail ended and there was nothing left between her and the stars. The moon was so big and beautiful that it made her ache, and as she sat there gazing in wonder, she opened her mouth and out came a moan. The moan turned into a howl. It echoed down through the canyons and gorges of the Pyrenees, and the whole world stopped to listen. The puppy grew up, and when she had children of her own, she taught them what she had learned, and to this day," he wagged a finger, "you can still hear a howl from time to time. You will hear it high in the mountains, where wolves still roam and where the wind likes to blow. Sometimes you can even hear it in your dreams, and then you will know." He gave her a hug and kissed the top of her head. "You will know that you too have a voice, and that you will find it again when the time is right."

Magdalena started to cry, then, and couldn't stop. When the pain in her chest finally subsided and she could brush aside the veil of tears, she found that the kitchen was empty. Dirty plates still sat on the table, but the chairs were vacant. Even her mother was gone, and a cool breeze seemed to snake along the floor, as if a door stood open somewhere. Her father's arm was still around her waist, though by now it was damp, and his head rested against hers, which still lay on his shoulder. His eyes were closed, and she would never forget the rise and fall of his chest as he breathed.

◆   ◆   ◆

THE STORY OF THE WOLF puppy was still fresh on Magdalena's mind when the Cathars returned to the Laux farm. They had come years before, and Magdalena remembered them as faces like pale moons and little bursts of excitement. The Cathars had come all the way from the Pyrenees of her father's youth, tracking him down like hounds trail a rabbit, to remind him of who he was and of the faith his mother had cherished. At the time, he'd had no interest in what they had to say, but now they were back—this time to see the red-haired girl who was said to be unusual, if not downright peculiar.

There were three of them, with heads of unruly hair and gray robes tied at the waist. Magdalena especially liked Timothy, a reedy man with a long neck and an Adam's apple that bobbed when he laughed, which was more often than not. Margaret, on the other hand, was the serious one, a mother hen who wanted to tuck stray souls under her feathers. She assured the troubled girl that the reason she so often felt out of place was because she was special. Magdalena looked so much like her grandmother that Margaret wondered aloud if a piece of the beloved parfaite's soul had awakened in her. The third Cathar, Isabelle, seemed to have no doubt that this was the case and looked at the child with eyes that glowed like lanterns.

Not everyone, however, was sanguine about the Cathars' visits and Magdalena could hear her parents' muffled voices at night, while she huddled in the refuge of her bed. She had at one time shared the room with Catharine, back before her sister left to live with her husband in the doomed château, which some called a castle and others a travesty, sitting as it did on the edge of the rough-and-tumble frontier.

"I don't like the influence these people are having on our daughter," Beatrice fretted.

"I don't much care for it, either," Pierre murmured.

"How do we know it's not of the devil?"

"Try to get some rest," Pierre said, in the weary tone he used when his wife worried a subject to death.

"Where exactly do they come from, anyway?"

"Who knows?" Pierre said, evasively. "They are a mystery even in the Pyrenees, where they used to abound."

"But why are they *here*?" Beatrice persisted.

Magdalena couldn't hear her father's response, but even at such a tender age, she thought she knew a thing or two. Penn's Woods was a special place, where anything was possible. Because of this, the English had come, the Swiss and the Dutch. The French had come, too, and, apparently, the Cathars, as well, albeit for reasons all their own.

◆ ◆ ◆

MAGDALENA'S SEARCH FOR ANSWERS WAS not limited to overhearing muted conversations in the night, and one evening, she watched her father with an eagle eye as he came in from the fields and washed his hands in the washbowl in the kitchen. She watched the strokes of the knife when he carved the roast and followed him into the living room after the meal. Magdalena normally had to help her mother with the cleanup and the dishes, and she prayed her mother would not seek her out.

Her father sat in his birchwood rocking chair in front of the unlit fireplace, brooding. She stood in front of him, waiting, and when he finally noticed her and gave a nod, she climbed up into his lap.

"What troubles my princess so?" he asked, his usual smile tugging at the corners of his mouth.

Magdalena looked up at him solemnly. After many long months of silence, she had found her voice again but had to choose her words carefully.

"Just the things that I have to think about," she said.

"Tell me, then," he offered, and at first she didn't respond.

But this was her chance, and she finally seized it.

"Why do men do bad things?" she wanted to know.

"Oh my, when you think about something, I better look out," he teased.

"I'm serious," she said, looking up at him earnestly. "Jean says it's because they are infected with evil," she went on, referring to her eldest brother, who, following Catharine's death, had come to the conclusion that the colony was no better than the places that the settlers had left behind, and let it be known that he intended to go to England, where the family had connections, to pursue a military career. "He says it is a disease like smallpox or measles, only much worse, and that some people are born with it."

"Jean has a unique way of looking at things. He has seen men at their worst and can no longer see them any other way."

"Andrew says he doesn't have time to waste on such thoughts," she said of her middle brother, who ran the sawmills owned by Lawrence Kraymer, who was Catharine's widower.

"I see you've been busy," Pierre chided. "I suppose you've asked Georgie, too, what he thinks on the matter?"

Magdalena's mouth twitched.

"Oh, you know Georgie. What's the use in asking him anything that doesn't have to do with that girl in Watertown? Ugh—I can't imagine why he's so interested in . . . you know . . ." she said, thinking of Georgie kissing the girl. She shuddered. "It's very disturbing if you ask me."

Pierre started to laugh, but she cut him short, returning to the question that perturbed her. "But just because you don't want to think about something doesn't make it go away, does it? If there is an Evil One, like the old Cathars said, and we just ignored him, that wouldn't be much of a hindrance to him, would it?"

"What matters is what's here," Pierre said, tapping her gently on the chest. His warmth seemed to envelop her, and she closed her eyes and tried to relax. But it was no use. Her father smelled of sunshine on fresh hay, and a new pain crawled up in her, the question of what she would do without him. What she would do without any of them, but especially this strong, warm human being in whose lap she huddled.

◆　◆　◆

THE QUESTION SHE HAD ASKED her father would not go away and continued to prick at her. She remembered the trial of the man who'd been arrested for taking Catharine and her baby from them. Magdalena could still see him sitting in the defendant's chair, large and slumping, his eyes sagging like overripe apples and his mouth hanging open, one minute bellowing hoarsely that he was an innocent man, unjustly wronged, and the next sobbing and begging for mercy. Magdalena had sat between her parents in a courtroom packed with farmers who smelled of the animals they worked with. Reaching over, she grasped her father's big, calloused hand and gripped it tightly.

Later, when they were back at the farmhouse, she asked her mother, "Why do people do bad things when they know they will get caught and have to cry about it?"

Beatrice stood at the kitchen counter, peeling potatoes for the supper, and Magdalena perched on a stool at her side, her youthful face earnest. Dappled sunlight played through the windows and a cool breeze swept along the floor.

"Humph—just don't you worry about Gus McDonall. The Good Lord will deal with him proper and put him straight to hell where he belongs," Beatrice said.

"But what if there isn't a hell, like Papa says?" Magdalena said.

"Oh, there's a hell all right," Beatrice assured her. "Your father knows a lot about a lot of things, but he doesn't know everything," she said, and again, Magdalena paused, wondering if what her mother had just said was true. She had never stopped to consider that her father didn't know everything there was to know and might even be wrong from time to time.

But in the end, her father's shortcomings didn't seem to matter very much. For the old wanderers in the woolen robes visited the farm time and again. They leaned on shepherds' staffs, walking barefoot, their feet so thick and heavy with callouses that they left footprints like boot marks in the dust. She knew full well that her father had little patience for them, but they had one thing that both of her parents seemed to lack. They had the answers she sought.

◆　◆　◆

THE MONTHS AND YEARS THAT followed were consumed with the rebuilding of Lawrence Kraymer's château. Magdalena was no longer a child, but had turned into a striking young woman, with a mind of her own. She did not understand sex and had no interest in it whatsoever. But she thought she understood love and knew that Catharine's death had wounded Lawrence grievously. Magdalena could still see it in him, the brokenness and pain. He could restore the château. But he could never restore his former life, and he lived alone in the imposing, haunted structure, where the wraiths of his wife and child wandered the halls at night.

"I think that Lawrence and I must marry," she announced, chopping at a weed that crowded a stalk of maize. Her mother, who worked nearby, looked at her in surprise.

"My goodness, first you want to be a Cathar and now this. Are you daft? Did you fall out of bed and hit your head on something?"

Magdalena rolled her eyes.

"Oh, Ma," she said. "The one doesn't have anything to do with the other." But then she had to pause to think about what she had just said. For, truly, the two things *could* be interrelated, she had to admit. As a grieving widower, Lawrence had shown no interest in other women, and as a Cathar, Magdalena had no interest in traditional marriage. However, marriage could serve purposes other than procreation, she reasoned.

"What would people say?" Beatrice fretted.

Magdalena cocked her head in thought.

"What do they say now?" she wanted to know, and this put her mother on the spot, for most people in the Watertown area saw Lawrence as a tragic figure. Many families had flawed children or broken relatives hidden away, and some feared Lawrence was one of these, a wealthy man successful in business but doomed by love. As for Magdalena, they had whispered about her ever since she was little, saying she was someone to watch out for, and not in a good way.

"People will talk—you know how they are," Beatrice finally said, avoiding her daughter's probing gaze.

Magdalena hesitated.

"And that's a concern of yours?" she said.

"Well, yes—I mean, no," Beatrice said, flustered.

"Mother . . ."

"I know—you'll do what you want," Beatrice sighed, going back to her weeding.

"I think it's a good idea and so does Lawrence. He wants to run for the assembly and being married helps his chances of getting elected. We've already discussed it. And as for me, if Lawrence and

I were married, maybe some of the boys would leave me alone. They can be such a bother sometimes. They think they can tell me what to do, and I won't have it!"

"If you've already made up your mind, then why come to me about it?" Beatrice said, irritably.

"Because I want your blessing."

Beatrice stopped hoeing. She leaned on the long handle, and her gaze drifted to where some of the old, native sentinel oaks stood alone in a landscape that was now mostly cleared. Magdalena wanted to reach out and touch her but instead waited, steeling herself to the possibility that she and her mother had less and less in common as the years passed.

Beatrice sighed, as if letting go of a notion that no longer served her. "I guess if I was really worried about what other people thought, I'd have done something about it a long time ago," she finally admitted.

And that was it. That was the big announcement about a nuptial that was bound to change everything. It was one of those days that separated the past from the future, in such a way that one could look back on it with the full realization that nothing thereafter would ever be the same.

Back in the environs of Toulouse, a youth who called himself Gabriel walked on the rutted road leading out of town. He liked the name, because someone once told him that Gabriel was an angel, and you couldn't get much better than that. Being a girl would have been much more difficult, he reasoned, because she might have been accosted by anyone. Boys had it better, if only a little, and Gabriel feigned a layer of toughness, so that those few people he couldn't avoid would give him a wide berth.

Once he got away from the houses, he felt better, but it wasn't until all signs of human habitation were gone, and he was alone on the dusty road, surrounded by yellow grass and scraggly bushes, and the trees, of course, that he actually breathed easier. Trees amazed him, because they were able to leave the ground and reach for the sky, with its distant, puffy clouds. The clouds seemed unfettered in a way he couldn't quite imagine, sailing along so high in the air that nothing could touch them.

Now and then, he would get a funny feeling, a ripple of fear that he had not paid close enough attention, and he would whirl around to see if anyone was there. The police would be looking for a burglar carrying two candlesticks. Silver candlesticks. Items worth so much that a penniless thief could never do anything with them on his own, and maybe not even with the help of another. In truth, Gabriel hadn't stolen them for their value. He'd taken them because the man who owned them would miss them sorely.

Opening the sack that he carried, he took out one of the candlesticks and looked down at it in disgust. Stepping to the side of the road, he cocked his arm back to throw it. But just then, he spotted an old man sitting on a nearby rock. The man sat with his elbows on his knees and his head hanging down, and Gabriel might not have even seen him if he hadn't stepped off the road himself.

He shoved the candlestick back into the sack, hoping to slip past the traveler unnoticed, but the *vieux* happened to look up and their eyes met. The stare, coming from such sunken eyes in the broad, bony face, froze Gabriel to the spot, and he didn't know what to do. His mouth went dry and he felt as if he somehow had a pine cone lodged in his throat.

Feigning nonchalance, he gave a stiff nod.

"*Bonjour,*" he said.

The old man's eyes seemed to be working as they peered at his face.

"I didn't tell them anything," the old man insisted, as if making an important point. "They tricked me. I would never betray her. Never!"

Gabriel studied him, suspiciously.

"I don't know what you're talking about," he said.

"You've got to believe me!"

Shaking his head, Gabriel sat down not far away and placed his sack on the ground. Careful to angle it so the old man could not see inside, he reached in and pulled out a piece of salami and the kind of knife that might be used in a kitchen to peel apples or turnips. He cut off a piece of the salami and held it out.

The old man looked at the offering and then gave a little jerk, as if something had moved inside of him. He accepted the salami, then sat there looking down at it. Raising it to his nose, he gave a long sniff before slipping it into his mouth. As he chewed, his eyes closed. Then he raised the hand and sniffed each finger, before licking them one by one.

"I haven't had anything this good in a very long time," he said, solemnly.

"Look, you must have some people who look after you," Gabriel said. The old man's plight pricked him hard, and he tried not to care. Everyone had someone, he consoled himself. But even those that did might wish that they didn't, a little, persistent voice countered.

"It's not good for a vieux to be all alone on a road like this," he added, trying to avoid thinking of his own predicament. "There are bad people and wild animals and who knows what else. You shouldn't be all by yourself."

He stood up and might have continued on his way. But something about the old man had struck a chord. The kind of note only certain people could hear. People such as a lad who had, himself, seen hard times.

"Why don't I walk with you for a bit?" he said. "It's not good to stay in one place for too long," he added, throwing an anxious glance back the way he had come.

The old man pondered this, then reached for a staff that lay nearby and got to his feet. He was a lot taller than Gabriel had expected, with broad shoulders that had obviously once been muscular. He wore simple peasants' clothes, but they looked new, which was curious.

"Do you happen to have more salami?" he asked, and Gabriel gave a quick nod.

"Sure," he said, fishing a piece of the preserved meat out of his sack as they walked.

They hadn't gone far, however, when nature called in a bothersome way. Gabriel had seen men take out their floppy parts and make water wherever they pleased, and it made him shudder. He sought privacy in the roadside bushes, while the old man continued on, alone. His fellow traveler appeared to have forgotten all about him, which was both a comfort and an irritation.

Indeed, Gabriel was thinking that his companion was a waste of time and that he might as well forget about him, too, when he saw flashes of movement on the road through the trees. Two men approached on horseback. They appeared to be soldiers and were closing fast on a traveler who had no idea they were there. A fugitive himself, Gabriel had a decision to make and not much time to make it.

The horsemen caught up with the old man, and one of them leaned sideways in his saddle to give him a long, hard look.

"What's your business on this road?" the soldier demanded, the gruff timbre of his voice traveling through the still morning air. He had the florid face of one who drank too much, and his clothes looked like he had slept in them. A jay flew from a nearby tree, crying out in alarm.

The old man seemed unaffected by the assault of such authority. "Whatever it is, it's none of yours," he replied.

"A beggar with an attitude!" the soldier sneered, shooting a glance at his companion.

In response, the old man planted his feet and held his staff with both hands, as if fully intending to use it as a weapon, in spite of the futility, not to mention the consequences, of doing so. He had the resolve of someone who had been pushed too far and would not be budged any further.

"What has my grandfather done now?" Gabriel piped, and the soldiers turned in their saddles. Gabriel had hidden his sack and sauntered up to them empty-handed. The soldiers exchanged looks.

"We're looking for a man who fits his description," said the one who hadn't yet spoken.

"He's mostly harmless," Gabriel assured him, apologetically. "He talks in his sleep, if that's a crime. And he chews with his mouth open. I keep telling him that if he's lucky enough to have something to eat, he should keep his mouth shut so that it doesn't fall out!"

The two soldiers again exchanged glances. One shook his head and the other grunted in disgust.

"Looks like we're wasting our time," one spat.

"The one we seek must be farther down the road," the other suggested.

"If he even came this way in the first place," the first suggested, as if they had in fact already discussed the matter. They eyed the old man and boy one last time, then one dug in his heels. His horse took off at a canter, and the other soldier quickly followed.

The old man watched them go, then turned an appraising eye upon the boy.

"That was a pretty sly thing you did," he said.

Gabriel flushed.

"I was just trying to help," he replied, with a tone that warned the other not to make too much of the gesture or take it for granted in any way.

The old man nodded solemnly. He opened his mouth as if intending to put the lad in his place—for that was Gabriel's experience with men. They thought so highly of themselves, thought they knew so much, that they had little time for a mere child. The priest, in particular, had often reminded Gabriel that his lot was to be seen and not heard, and not even seen unless beckoned.

Then the old man spoke, in a most surprising way.

"Thank you," he said.

No one had ever thanked Gabriel before, and much as he tried to suppress it, he felt like a lark carried aloft by a sudden breeze. His second thoughts about having helped the old man vanished, and he yearned to know just who his companion was.

◆　◆　◆

GABRIEL HADN'T INTENDED TO SPEND much time in the company of someone who would hobble his progress, but one thing simply led to another. He learned the vieux had been away from home for a very long time and that his name was Jean-Pierre, which was somewhat interesting, inasmuch as hyphenated names carried a whiff of nobility. But getting the information was not easy, as Jean-Pierre seemed so lost in an inner world. It took a lot of prodding, and Gabriel wearied of the effort.

He thought of parting ways and striking out on his own, but the temperature started to drop, and the tunic that had smothered him in the midday heat now felt like cold metal against his skin. The long shadows of twilight began to creep through the trees, making him anxious. For though Gabriel had spent plenty of nights alone—and indeed preferred it that way—he had never spent a night outdoors, where the wolf and the badger lived. He had never had to find shelter where there wasn't one ready-made, and he had never had to sleep on the ground, where the snakes and spiders crawled.

"Don't you think we should stop for the night, while it's still light enough to see?" he asked, and Jean-Pierre seemed puzzled by the question. He seemed torn between necessity and whatever it was that drove him forward.

Gabriel took the lack of response as agreement, for who could argue with the advancing night? The sun dipped below the horizon and the deepening shadows now seemed like a darkening pool of cold water. Gabriel had brought along a fire-starter, more out of luck than forethought. But he had never actually used one, and the sparks he showered on dry leaves and pinecones didn't even make a puff of smoke.

"You need tinder," said the old man, sitting stiffly on a nearby rock.

"If you know so much, you can pitch in and help," Gabriel retorted.

"You need dry moss or shredded bark," Jean-Pierre said, but otherwise showed no sign of budging.

By now, the cold crawled down Gabriel's neck and up his sleeves, and he searched with increasing urgency for something to get the fire going. He found some dried mushrooms stuck to the side of a log but passed them by. Then he found a partially hollowed tree that had been struck by lightning. A dry, fluffy litter lay inside, and he gathered it up and carried it back to the campsite.

Now when he struck the fire-starter, the sparks caught, and a flame rapidly spread. But the pieces of wood he had gathered were too large, and the fire died out without igniting them.

"You need kindling," the old man said, and Gabriel had to clench his teeth to bite back a response.

He hurriedly gathered more tinder and then a pile of twigs and bark—anything that looked small enough to quickly burn. This time, when he made sparks, the tinder caught, and the kindling began to smoke. An orange tongue of flame leaped up through the twigs, and Gabriel feverishly added larger pieces of wood lest the fire die out again. His heart surged when one of the bigger pieces began to burn, and before long, he had a crackling fire going.

He shot a triumphant look at his companion, but Jean-Pierre seemed lost in thought. The firelight flickered on his craggy face. When Gabriel roused him to share some cheese and the last of the salami, Jean-Pierre winced as if a bubble of pain had risen through his large, emaciated frame.

"When we get to the manoir, I shall return your kindness," he said, and Gabriel felt a spurt of excitement at this new clue to his companion's identity. He had no idea what a manoir was, but it sounded bigger than the priest's mansion. It certainly sounded grander than the modest home where he, himself, had been born and lived, until the hot, thirsty day when the priest left the Compostela Trail to seek out the well in Gabriel's village.

"This manoir you speak of—is that where we're headed?" he asked.

But the old man only lapsed into silence again, as if words took a toll on what little strength he had left. Many were the times Gabriel had relied on a good story to get him through the night, and so, now, beside the fire, he began to make one up. Even though he still knew very little about his fellow traveler, he now had enough to imagine him to be a king in shabby clothes, on his way to his castle, where a faithful and persevering wife awaited him. During his long absence, her hair had grown unshorn until it touched the ground, and she waited because true love endured. Gabriel imagined the king had children who waited by their mother's side. The boy wore a suit of armor, because true love was a treasure that needed defending, and the girl carried a bow and a quiver of arrows, because in Gabriel's telling, girls did not just sit around waiting to be kissed by somebody. They were as strong as the boys they could have been, under different circumstances, and true love required every bit of strength you had. It demanded that you stand your ground and never give up.

With nothing else to do to pass the time, Gabriel sank into a daydream that lasted long into the night, long past the withering point of the old man's words, past the last efforts of the dying fire, past even the fading glow of the coals that popped and hissed and finally lay spent. Leaning against a rock, Jean-Pierre was just another of the many shadows, and then, when the cold came in with a vengeance—as Gabriel had known it would—he nevertheless felt warmed, first by his imaginings and then by the thin lines that his arms made against his ribs. Drifting to sleep, he dreamed that if one such as the aged traveler could turn out to be so special, then he, too, could rise like a waif who discovered the prince he was meant to be.

———•———

Gabriel woke with a shudder as a pale, unforgiving light crept across the land. He glanced over at the inert shape of his companion. During the night, Jean-Pierre had let out a yelp, like a kicked dog, and then, sometime later, moaned loudly with each breath. Now, Gabriel crawled over to him and peered at his face. He held the back of his hand to the old man's nose, seeking any warmth or the flutter of breath. Satisfied that the gaunt figure was still alive, he stood up and looked around, as the features of the landscape slowly separated from the cloak of darkness.

The sun had not yet risen, and Gabriel shivered uncontrollably. Searching his sack, he found a hard lump of bread. His stomach twisted with hunger, but a glance at the sleeping man made him sigh, shake his head, and leave the food alone.

A crow cawed insistently in a nearby tree, and Gabriel knitted together the resolve it would take to face the day ahead. Moving helped to warm him, and he thought he might walk along the road a ways. Reaching down, he picked up a stone—just the right size for throwing, he thought, which would limber up his arm and chase some of the chill and stiffness from his body. He aimed at a tree, and the throw went wide—rather like a girl would throw, he noted to himself, unhappily.

He picked up another stone and bounced it in his palm, resolving to do better. By now, the sun was up and a swath of yellow light cut through the roadside brush, the trees, and anything else that dared to stand in its path. Something emerged from the shadows. Then, a hare sat upright, its ears catching the light and its nose twitching. Dropping down, it sniffed at a blade of grass and snipped it off at the ground, apparently oblivious to the boy who stood nearby. Normally, Gabriel might have just watched. But a hare made a far more interesting target than a tree, and he gave the stone a couple more bounces and then let fly.

What happened next was unthinkable. The stone arced. But rather than going wide, as Gabriel had expected, it struck the hare, which made a leap and then fell on its side, legs kicking.

Gabriel cried aloud in dismay. And then matters only got worse, for when he spun around, right there, behind him, stood the old man. Their eyes locked, and Gabriel felt his face start to crumple.

"Good throw," Jean-Pierre said, which only served to make matters worse.

"I didn't mean it," Gabriel said. Tears darted to his eyes.

Jean-Pierre studied him gravely. But just then, a muffled cacophony rebounded through the wooded area, shattering the stillness. A brightly colored, enclosed caravan approached, bringing with it the sounds of a groaning axle, metal-rimmed wheels that snapped stones and sent them skittering, and the clatter and jangle of pots and pans. The woman who sat on the bench wore a dark scarf on her head. She had smears of ash under her eyes and large hoop earrings. Pulling on the reins and applying the hand brake, she eyed the foot-travelers.

Finally, she gestured with her chin toward the dead animal.

"Is that yours?" she asked.

"Who wants to know?" Jean-Pierre said, regarding her suspiciously. The woman snorted.

"The Queen of Sheba, that's who! And who might you be, if you don't mind my asking?"

The old man drew himself up to his full height.

"I am Seigneur Jean-Pierre du Laux," he said, and the woman's eyes widened. She gave another snort, then threw back her head and laughed outright. Her ample bosoms shook. The long skirt she wore over her splayed knees quivered.

"Fair enough," she sighed. She looked at the boy with merriment, as if wondering what title he might claim. Then, glancing once more at the hare, she gestured, reluctantly, toward the bench beside her.

"Okay, a good laugh is worth something, I guess. Climb aboard, then, if you want . . . *seigneur.* Just be sure to bring that there critter with you." She jerked her chin toward the hare.

Jean-Pierre studied her for a moment, perhaps weighing his options. But a vehicle to ride in had undeniable advantages, and he reached for the rail. The conveyance sagged under his weight. The woman's eyes rolled suggestively from her passenger to the dead animal that still lay along the road.

"Aren't you forgetting something?" she prodded.

"I'll get it," Gabriel said.

Swiping at his face with the back of a hand, he hastened to pick up the fallen creature. Again the tears started to come. It was getting downright annoying, and he was relieved that his back was to the others. Boys didn't cry, he told himself. They carried little men inside of them and endured hardships like horses withstood the cold of a winter day. They soldiered forth, facing the challenges that came their way, and Gabriel had no illusions as to the obstacles he faced. He would have to get a lot better at being who he pretended to be if he didn't want people to find out who he really was.

◆　◆　◆

THE GYPSY WOMAN, WHOSE NAME was Sara, lost little time in making camp. She pulled the wagon to a halt in the shade of an ash tree, then climbed down, groaning at every move her body made. Placing a hand on her hip, she winced as she straightened up.

"I would say don't grow old . . ." she muttered, her half-lidded eyes darting to the boy.

A thought seemed to land in her mind, like a crow settling onto one of the branches of an oak. Still grumbling under her breath, she walked around the wagon, shooting another quick glance at the boy before climbing into the back. Pots clattered as she rummaged about. Then, her head poked back into view.

"Don't just stand there," she said. "While I'm finding something to cook with, somebody's got to gather wood and get a fire going. Go on, now. Make yourself useful if you expect to eat!"

Meanwhile, Jean-Pierre climbed down from the wagon and stood next to it, clearly unhappy with the delay. Ignoring him, Sara tied the hare's head to a corner of the wagon and proceeded to cut the skin around the neck with a small knife. She ran the blade down the length of its back to the tail. Then, setting the knife aside, she grasped the two collar flaps of skin and pulled the hide from the animal in one smooth motion. She eviscerated the hanging carcass, saving the heart and liver, then untied it and laid it on the back gate of the wagon, where she proceeded to cut it into pieces.

Gabriel collected dried moss and kindling and soon got a fire going. Meanwhile, Sara fetched a pot from the wagon. The sizzle of meat soon followed. Sara prodded the pieces of hare with a wooden spoon, then added a carrot and a handful of wild onions. She added a bladder of red wine and gave the pot a stir.

"When God gives you a hare, it's time to eat," she said, glancing again at Gabriel.

Gabriel didn't respond. He was far more concerned with Jean-Pierre, who stood muttering to himself and thrusting his staff at the ground, as if stabbing the life out of ants.

"You ever eat hare before?" Sara asked.

Gabriel gave her a blank look.

"You'll thank me for it," she assured him.

But he had already turned away, a hard, painful lump forming in his chest. The aroma of cooking meat did indeed make him ache with hunger. But he couldn't get the sight out of his head—an animal minding its own business, innocently chewing a blade of grass, with no idea of the misfortune heading its way. It certainly hadn't asked for it, any more than Gabriel had asked for the hardships he, himself, had endured over the past several years.

When the meal was ready, Sara spooned a large portion onto Gabriel's plate. The portion she gave Jean-Pierre was much smaller, and she thrust it at him begrudgingly, as if the hare had been hers to begin with. Jean-Pierre sniffed at his plate, then lifted a piece of meat with his fingers and sniffed again.

He placed his uneaten meal on the tailgate of the caravan.

"We're wasting time," he said.

Sara rolled her eyes.

"You have someplace better to be?" she growled. When he didn't respond, she pressed on, "Let me remind you who's driving this caravan. *I'm* the one in charge of where we go and when we'll get there. If you don't like it . . ."

She jerked her chin toward the open road, and Jean-Pierre regarded her solemnly for a moment, then nodded. He glanced at Gabriel, who felt the tug of his gaze. Then, he poked at the ground with his staff and lifted his chin, a faraway look in his eyes. Without bidding farewell, he started to walk.

Sara lurched to her feet and glared at the departing figure. Then, she turned to Gabriel, as if pleading innocence concerning any offense Jean-Pierre might have taken and, in no small measure, gauging the youth's reaction. But Gabriel thrust aside his plate and dashed after his aged friend, and swearing under her breath, Sara rushed to clean up the pot and dishes.

◆　◆　◆

AT SOME POINT IN THE journey, even Gabriel wondered where they were headed. It was one thing to humor an old man when the future was still something broad and unformed and the miles ahead were little more than a tease. It was another, entirely, when the distance traveled could be measured in the pain of a jolting ride and each fork in the road required a decision that became a point of no return.

Sara seemed none too happy. Whenever she cast her eyes upon Gabriel, he felt as if fleas had gotten into his clothing, and he was uneasily aware of the fact that he somehow factored into whatever choices she made. She had let it be known that she wanted to head south, where she intended to join an encampment of her people. But Jean-Pierre had countered that his destination lay elsewhere, with or without the convenience of a caravan, and Gabriel, torn betwixt and between, sided with the old man.

Sara was still visibly stewing on the predicament she'd found herself in, when the road topped a rise and then dropped into a dark patch of woods. She yanked on the reins and set the brake.

"Enough of this," she said. She stabbed her finger at the woods. "I'm not going any further, and I'm certainly not going anywhere near that accursed place. They say the devil lives there. A whole army of men died in those trees, and they say the devil ate their souls." She turned a hard look on Jean-Pierre, as if she had been more than accommodating and daring him to say otherwise.

Jean-Pierre gazed at the woods with haunted eyes. Taking a deep breath, he glanced heavenward, then gripped the siderail and got down from the wagon.

"What do you think you're doing?" Sara demanded. But Jean-Pierre now seemed unaware of her. As he gazed at the woods, tears bubbled and spilled down his cheeks.

Gabriel jumped from the wagon and crept to the old man's side.

"And you! Where do you think you're going?" Sara cried. "The both of you are crazy!"

But Jean-Pierre had already started down the hill, with Gabriel at his side. He leaned on the youth's small shoulder, while the other hand wielded the staff.

"Dear mother of God," Gabriel heard Sara exclaim behind them as the woods loomed.

The grove was unbearably still. Dark, twisted tree trunks and leafless branches snaked among the other foliage, as if some disease had taken its toll, causing death and deformity. The smell of rotting walnuts and moldering loam lay heavily along a creek that now looked like little more than a seepage. The birdsong one might have expected in such a place was absent, along with the clouds of insects that normally would have called it home.

Jean-Pierre stood as if transported to another time and place.

"Is something the matter?" Gabriel asked, anxiously.

Jean-Pierre's fingers flexed like bony talons on the boy's shoulder.

"Are you okay?" Gabriel persisted.

But just then, Sara's caravan banged and clattered down the hill and into the gloomy woods, where it hurtled past them without slowing. Jean-Pierre flexed his fingers a final time, then dropped his arm to his side, and without thinking, Gabriel slipped his small hand into the much bigger one. He gazed up earnestly at the towering figure. Jean-Pierre hesitated, as if the spell of the woods was too powerful to resist. His head turned, his eyes casting about. His tongue shot out to moisten his lips and then the head drooped. He might have stood there forever but for the gentle pressure in his palm.

Sunlight enveloped them as they emerged from the woods, and Gabriel was amazed to see the caravan waiting in the middle of the road, its red and green paint making an unexpected splash of color. He'd been sure he would never see the conveyance again, and yet here it stood, like an abandoned shack on wooden wheels, the summer heat radiating around it.

◆　◆　◆

Gabriel was relieved Sara had not driven off and left them behind, for he truly didn't know what he and Jean-Pierre would have done without her. But he was no longer fooled. For the first time in his young life, he was able to see some of the cunning behind the decisions that people made, and he was not deceived by Sara's benevolence. When she looked at Jean-Pierre, he was certain she saw a frail old man who was a liability but who most likely wouldn't be around much longer. In Gabriel she saw a youth who had formed an attachment to the vieux but who would most likely be on his own soon enough. She tolerated the one due to the interesting prospects offered by the other, which made Gabriel fear that he had merely traded one captor for another.

And looking at Jean-Pierre in this light, he smarted. The old man did not deserve such disregard, and Gabriel rued that Jean-Pierre was no longer the vital person he had obviously once been. He felt a growing regret for the man's weakness, his decline, and the dubious future that seemed to lie in wait for the both of them. For by now, the two had become so intertwined, in Gabriel's mind, that he could not see himself without the other, not now and maybe not ever.

Someone like Sara would never understand this, he thought, as the caravan trundled along. Her resentment seethed like the steam that rose from a simmering pot. But he had made his decision, and if Jean-Pierre were to die, as Sara obviously thought he soon would, and if Gabriel were to end up in her care, as he feared he might, he determined that he would steal off into the night once more, the same as he had done with the priest, who had cared for him like a farmer cares for a lamb he has raised for the slaughter.

Lost in thoughts such as these, Gabriel failed to see the view that opened up as the caravan crested yet another of the many rolling hills. The first indication that something was afoot was the way Sara stiffened as she jerked on the reins. Following her frozen gaze, he saw an enormous edifice on the plain below, a veritable castle, with a crenellated wall that looked like it could withstand an army.

Jean-Pierre leaned forward with frightening intensity and gestured impatiently. "Don't stop."

"That's the manoir you've been talking about?" Sara gasped.

"*Allez!*" Jean-Pierre said.

And that was when the real fear started, the apprehension that Jean-Pierre either was indeed a seigneur, which still made no sense, or that he was an imposter of such grand proportions that he endangered the lives of everyone around him. There were certain things that even Gabriel knew a body didn't do, and hauling a Gypsy wagon to the door of a nobleman's abode was one of them.

"Allez, allez!" Jean-Pierre shouted, stabbing a finger toward the manoir, and Sara let the wagon roll, not because she wanted to—that much was clear—but because she had come this far and didn't know what else to do.

It quickly became obvious, however, that something was wrong. The moat that surrounded the wall was overgrown with tall weeds, which wouldn't have been a cause for alarm in and of itself, as moats had long since fallen out of style and were generally no longer maintained. Of more immediate concern, though, the gate stood open. The top hinge appeared to have given way, allowing the heavy wooden door to sag. Inside the yard, dandelions, chickweed, and thistle grew waist high. The front door of the imposing home was boarded shut, as were the tall windows on the ground level, and the house had the spent stillness of a corpse.

The caravan stopped, and with a burst of youthful agility, Jean-Pierre leaped to the ground and dashed to the front door. He ran his hands over the rough, splintery boards, then, stepping back, glanced up at the shuttered windows of the second story.

"El?" he whimpered, then let out a mighty bellow. "Eleanor?"

Rushing to a window, he grasped a board that was nailed over it and yanked. But the board held, and he dashed around a corner of the house. Soon there came the screech of yielding nails and breaking glass, and Sara turned a crazed look on Gabriel.

"We have to get out of here," she croaked, jerking the reins in a way that confused the horse, which bolted sideways and broke one of the wooden hames attached to its collar. The horse shied and bolted the other way, while Sara struggled for control.

"What are you doing?" Gabriel cried.

"People who live in houses like that don't care about people like us," she said, throwing a frightened look over her shoulder. "If anyone catches us here, they will hang us. The *maréchaussée* will hang all three of us from the trees!" she said, referring to soldiers who were temporarily unassigned to their accustomed military duties, and who acted as a roving police force, with full authority to dispense justice as they saw fit.

"But what about Jean-Pierre? We can't leave him!"

"We have to go!" Sara shouted, slapping down hard with the reins, and Gabriel leaped free of the conveyance. He sprawled face down on the ground, then scrambled to his feet, only to topple once again. Throwing the boy a savage look, Sara appeared to have a moment of indecision. Her frozen visage made for a frightening apparition. Then she whipped the horse, and the caravan thundered off through the broken gate, the pots and pans clanging in a riot of sound that grew fainter and fainter until an eerie silence once again filled the yard.

Gabriel got to his feet and brushed himself off, wiping at the dirt and broken weed stems that clung to his tunic and pants. The manoir loomed with a deadly silence, and he followed the perimeter until he found the window Jean-Pierre had broken. Blood smeared one of the glass shards that still clung to the frame, and Gabriel climbed up onto the outer sill and carefully stepped through. The room inside was empty. Even the carpets had been taken up, leaving pale areas on the aged flooring. Dust lay everywhere, and he followed the footprints Jean-Pierre had left behind, along with drops of wet blood.

He climbed the stairs, up through the musty gloom to the second floor, where he found Jean-Pierre collapsed in one of the bedrooms. Kneeling by the man's side, Gabriel placed a hand against the pale forehead and hovered it in front of the mouth. Having reassured himself that Jean-Pierre was still alive and that the cut was but a small one on the arm, he fretted over what to do next. He glanced around the room, looking for anything he could use to make Jean-Pierre more comfortable, but all he saw was a woman's dresser with a cracked mirror, and a bed frame that had been stripped of its mattress. The other rooms were equally bare. So, he went downstairs, hoping to at least find some food to offer Jean-Pierre when he roused—assuming he would. But the house had been ransacked, and Gabriel found only broken jars in the kitchen and empty wine racks in the basement.

Beside himself with frustration, Gabriel went out into the yard. The sun baked down hard, despite the late season, with autumn on the way, and the dry air seemed to clutch at his throat. Grasshoppers popped and clattered among the dry grass and thistles as he kicked his way to what appeared to be a barracks. Pushing the door open, he found only a small fireplace darkened with soot in a room that was otherwise empty. So, he went on to the stables, where he found only vacant stalls filled with matted straw. Even the horse tack had been taken.

Returning outside, he squinted in the sun, trying to decide what to do. That was when he noticed the towers on either side of the gate in the wall at the edge of the yard, and a thought occurred to him. Thrusting his shins through the scraggly chickweed that carpeted the ground, he went to the door at the base of one of the towers. The heavy iron hinges made cracking sounds as he pushed, as if they had become frozen at some point lost to time. They yielded and he stepped into the gloom, batting at the spiderwebs that draped all around him. He climbed up a flight of stone steps that had been gullied by hundreds of years of use. There was no railing, and he had to place a hand against the wall for balance.

Splinters of light showed through the wooden door at the top of the stairway, and forcing it open, he stepped out onto the rampart. He leaned over the crenellated parapet. The land below dropped down to a river valley, and he spied a cluster of houses around a central square, where a market day appeared to be in progress.

Hastening from the tower, Gabriel made his way down to the village and to the market square, where he stood out like a stray cat among the crates of live ducks and chickens, baskets of eggs, and piles of bread loaves and cheeses. There were turnips and broad beans, greens and bunches of herbs. He knew he had to be careful, for suspicious stares followed his every move. Strangers were always suspect, and pity the migrant soul if a farmer broke a leg or a young bride miscarried her first child. But it was hard to be cautious when a sick man back at the manoir was in such desperate need, when his own stomach felt like a bag full of sharpened sticks, and when he had no money to pay for any of the abundance that surrounded him.

Then, he seemed to catch a break. One of the dogs that prowled the square got too close to a crated chicken. The bird squawked and flapped in panic, which drew curious looks, and Gabriel plucked a wedge of cheese from a nearby table and stuffed it under his tunic. Turning to flee, he ran right into a woman who stood with her hands on her hips, glaring at him. He tried to slip around her, but a heavy hand dropped on his shoulder. Twisting, he saw a young man with a curly beard and the grim features of one who understood full well what Gabriel was doing—and who had no sympathy for him whatsoever.

"Thief!" The woman pointed a finger, and the grip on Gabriel's shoulder tightened.

"Where do you think you're going?" the young man growled.

He took the cheese from Gabriel and handed it back to the woman. By now, other people were gathering round.

"Who is he?" someone asked.

"What're we going to do with him?" another wanted to know.

"I've got a barn we can lock 'im in," a voice piped up.

"Wait!" Gabriel cried, his brain working feverishly. For the past several weeks, he had relied on the cloak of deception to keep him safe. Truth had seemed to be an enemy, but now he saw it as his only option. "It's not for me. It's for an old man who is sick and may be dying. He says his name is Jean-Pierre. He says he's a seigneur!"

The grip on his shoulder relaxed a little. The excited voices quieted. People glanced at each other, no longer so sure of themselves and the situation as they'd been just moments ago.

"A seigneur, you say?" one voice ventured.

"Did he say Jean-Pierre?" a second queried.

"The seigneur? He's back?" said a third.

"I thought he was dead."

The crowd started to murmur.

The man with the curly beard scowled. "Where is this 'seigneur'?"

Gabriel hastened to explain that Jean-Pierre was at the manoir, where he had collapsed and needed help. The crowd exchanged uncomfortable looks, and some stared expectantly at the youth with the curly beard, as if what he might have to say mattered.

"Show us," the young man said, releasing his grip on Gabriel and giving him a shove. Gabriel rubbed his shoulder gingerly. He stole a longing glance at the cheese he had tried to purloin and which was now back on the merchant's table, but turned back the way he had come and led the way toward the turreted rooftop just visible in the distance. A score of people followed. A woman who had been watching from an open window burst from her door to join them, as did a man who pulled along the goat he'd meant to sell.

When they reached the manoir, Gabriel hung back as the crowd gathered before the porch. One of the villagers finally pushed the door open. Glancing behind him, as if seeking support, he entered the house. One and then another of the villagers followed, and soon the entire throng pushed inside.

The young man with the curly beard, who had remained at Gabriel's side, took a knife from his pocket and began to pare his fingernails, feigning disinterest in the manoir. He glanced at

Gabriel, as if warning him to stay put. But then a shriek came from the second floor, a cry of discovery that could only mean one thing.

"*Merde*," the youth breathed. He folded his knife, thrust it back in his pocket, and dashed inside.

Gabriel could have slipped away. But he stood as rooted to the spot as one of the nearby rose bushes, which looked wild and unkempt, but had persisted in spite of a lack of care and still clung to the soil with a tenacious grip. The world as Gabriel knew it swirled around him. It beckoned him to do something, anything, but he found he could do nothing at all.

◆   ◆   ◆

OVER THE NEXT COUPLE OF weeks, the manoir bustled with activity. Gabriel stayed out of the way. Mostly, he watched the goings-on from the window of the barracks. A bed had been provided from among the myriad of tables and chairs, lamps, carpets and tapestries that were being carted back to the manoir by villagers with rounded shoulders and downcast eyes.

For many long days, Jean-Pierre, whom Gabriel now reluctantly thought of as the seigneur, remained hidden from view, buried deep in the heart of a tragic manoir, and Gabriel didn't know if he still lived or had passed away. Gabriel could have marched up to the house and seen for himself, of course, but something held him back. Something pointed a finger at him and told him he didn't belong. The man he had befriended on the road turned out to be someone he didn't know, but it was more than that. There was the bald fact of his own deceit, which may have served a purpose, but now stood between him and any further companionship with the seigneur.

Turning away from the window, he looked around the barracks with dismay. For even a place such as this made him feel like an imposter. It was part of an estate to which he didn't belong. Part of a life so far outside the orbit of his personal existence that his mind clogged and faltered at the mere thought of it.

When the seigneur finally made an appearance, Gabriel was overjoyed. But this effervescence quickly soured, for he still faced the problem of what he would now do with himself.

The seigneur stood in the sun, talking to the youth with the curly beard. They stood face to face with heads inclined, in the manner of individuals having a serious conversation. The seigneur was the taller of the two, and he placed a hand on the other's shoulder, walking him toward the house, and Gabriel felt a stab of jealousy.

Later, a knock on the barracks door startled him, and he hastily rose from the bed where he had been lying. It was the seigneur, who no longer wore peasant clothes, but a blousy white shirt and tight-fitting breeches. He had exchanged his country sabots for the kind of riding boots that only a special kind of person wore.

The seigneur's expression was pained.

"Where have you been?" he asked.

Gabriel recoiled from the absurdity of the question. His eyes swam, seeking as much information as possible about the seigneur's well-being, and he was relieved that the man appeared to be in remarkably good health. But the gulf between them was just too wide, and Gabriel viewed the seigneur as if from a distant shore.

"I'm glad you are better," he mumbled, turning away with a heavily troubled heart.

The seigneur stepped across the barracks threshold as if he owned the place, which of course he did.

"I heard about you," the seigneur said, "going to the village and bringing help. You went to a lot of trouble on my behalf, and I am grateful. It is because of you that I am still standing."

"I didn't do nothin'," Gabriel said, shaking his head like a horse refusing the halter.

He suffered the seigneur's probing gaze. He might not have known who the seigneur really was, back when he appeared to be something else, but the seigneur didn't know him, either, he thought bitterly. The seigneur had no idea who it was that had taken refuge in his barracks.

"François and I are going to Pau to deal with some banking issues," the seigneur said. "I thought maybe you would come along. We could get you some new clothes," he suggested, no doubt thinking the boy would be pleased at the prospect.

"Who's François?" Gabriel asked, sullenly.

"It's a long story," the seigneur replied. His mouth hung open, as if he had momentarily slipped into a distant past. But then his jaw tightened, and he took a breath as if biting off a mouthful of air. "Look, we're leaving in the morning, and I would like you to come along. You'll like François. You can learn a lot from him, like I did from his father, a long time ago. It would be good for you to get to know him."

Gabriel stood with his shoulder to the seigneur, sometimes glancing at him but mostly looking away, and when the seigneur finally turned toward the door, it both relieved and pained him. He almost lurched after him. But there was the other thing, the big lie, that froze Gabriel where he stood as he watched the seigneur fill the doorframe and then proceed in the direction of the house. The big house. Nowhere that a vagabond like Gabriel could ever call home.

The day seemed to crawl. The afternoon slid into long shadows, with night following swiftly. After many sighs and sleepless hours, Gabriel finally rose and crept back to the window, where he had stood so often of late. A full moon spread a silver light on the yard and the towering manoir seemed dormant, as if momentarily thwarted in some way. Gabriel quickly found the sack he had brought with him from Toulouse, which still carried the heavy weight of the silver candlesticks. He stuffed an extra pair of socks into it, along with a blanket that one of the villagers had given him. When he stepped outside, the predawn cold hit him like a slap in the face.

The rising sun found him on a southerly road that wound into the Pyrenees. He knew about the pilgrims that thronged it on their way to visit some bones that were said to be those of a saint. But he had never really noticed the travelers before, back when he was too young to understand what a pilgrim was. Now, with new eyes, he saw the carts with drivers carrying whips, the occasional coach, and far more often, the clusters of men and women in simple country attire, some wearing bags with holes for arms and some walking barefoot, even though the nights were cold and they didn't appear to have the toughened bodies of ones used to a hard life. High above them, the ravens drifted with eyes bent toward the ground, as if keeping watch on the curious lot, and higher still, the buzzards circled.

The road threaded through one small village after another. The red-roofed homes had open windows, where residents leaned on the sills to watch the passing pilgrims, no doubt curious and perhaps just a little smug, Gabriel thought, that they had found the one place in the world where they belonged. This was their home, their village, where they ate and slept and *played*, and even as Gabriel thought it, the word struck him. For he couldn't remember ever having played—not the way boys who wanted to be men played at *boules*, while the younger ones waved sticks in the air as they battled their way to an imagined glory, or the way girls coddled dolls made of wood or sheep's tails. Thinking of such things, Gabriel felt a hole in his chest that the wind blew through.

At night, he spread out his blanket near one of the pilgrim campsites, not so close as to feel the heat and maybe draw the ire of anyone who cast a glance his way, but not so far away as to be swallowed by the darkness, either. Even as a youth, Gabriel knew of the things that crept about in the dark—highwaymen and miscreants and lurkers from nearby towns who roamed like packs of wolves—and he spent many an hour looking at the clutter of stars above, wondering if he would ever be safe again.

Sometimes, he fell in with a particular group and a pilgrim would share with him a piece of bread or a bit of cheese, even a swig of wine, if they thought the eye in the sky was watching. And on the fifth day, Gabriel came to a village that pricked his memory like an unhealed sore. Leaving the road, he entered the cluster of homes and came to the village square, where he had met the priest who had changed his life. The priest had smiled and asked him his name. He looked at Gabriel in a way no man had ever looked at him before, the eyes condescending yet probing. The lips pursing. The smell of the man's perfume plucked and cloyed.

The house still looked the same. Mud walls and a roof with red tiles, like the cottages around it. Open holes for windows where the heavy-bodied flies circled. A door that he hesitated in front of before knocking, feeling lost on the threshold of the place he'd once called home. The priest had accompanied him from the well. In retrospect, Gabriel knew his parents must have been terrified, but it didn't ease his pain or justify their readiness to give the priest exactly what he wanted.

A woman wearing a long dress and a black apron came to the door and peered out at him. Although old and wizened, she had the beauty of the husk of a flower that still stands in winter, and Gabriel didn't know whether to embrace her or to turn and run and run until the running was out of him and he fell to the earth and died. He smelled stewed vegetables and soot and the musty odor of farm animals.

"What do you want?" she asked, suspiciously, clutching a wooden spoon in her claw of a hand.

"*Ama*, it's me," Gabriel said.

The woman's eyes narrowed. Her knuckles whitened as she tightened her grip on the wooden spoon. She looked past Gabriel as if suspecting she were being tricked in some way and the devil himself was behind it all. Hating himself for the tears that bubbled, Gabriel choked back a sob.

"Ama, it's me—Gotzone," he said.

The woman recoiled.

"Gotzone?" she said. Her eyes worked him over. They went to the cropped hair, the tunic and heavily patched cotton pants. She clearly didn't understand what she saw, and her neck stiffened beneath her loose black shawl.

Her chin started to move before the words came out.

"You can't be Gotzone—you're a boy," she stammered, backing away and crossing herself.

"Ama, it's me—the girl you sold," Gotzone said.

NINE

Gotzone's mother, Arrosa, appeared stunned. She seemed suddenly lost in her own home, looking at the table and cooking hearth as if she had never seen them before. When Gotzone approached, she flinched and backed away, her eyes glazing as if she were trapped in another time, where decisions had been made with a finality that had once seemed irrevocable.

Without welcoming Gotzone, she nevertheless bade her enter, breathing shallowly. Arrosa seemed to wobble and Gotzone wondered if she might pass out. Lifting an arm, the older woman gestured woodenly about the house, which had one other room, a bedroom where the whole family slept. Glancing back at Gotzone, her gaze fixed on the clothes the girl wore.

"Come . . ." she said, turning toward the bedroom.

"Ama . . ."

"We have to get you changed before your father comes home. He can't see you like this."

Arrosa hesitated, her wrist against her forehead, then pulled a box out from under the bed. She removed a dress.

"Here, this should fit," she said.

"Ama, I don't want—"

"If he sees you in boys' clothes, I don't know what he would do!"

Arrosa grabbed hold of Gotzone's tunic and started pulling at it. She tugged down her daughter's pants and gasped.

"You're a woman now!" she exclaimed.

Gotzone placed a hand over her lower belly and tried hard not to jerk away. Her fear was palpable, never mind that Arrosa was her mother and used to wash her from a basin of soapy water. Then, with the dress finally over her head and in place, she felt better, more protected in some odd way, as if clothing—even a dress—were a form of armor. Arrosa moved jerkily as she fled the room, and Gotzone followed after, finding her mother sitting at the table with her face in her hands.

"I had to come here—I had nowhere else to go!" Gotzone tried to tell her. But Arrosa just shook her head, rubbing her face into her palms.

"You don't belong in this place anymore," Arrosa said.

"This is my home!"

"No . . . No . . ."

"Ama . . ."

"Don't call me that," Arrosa said, shuddering.

◆　◆　◆

EVEN THOUGH GOTZONE KNEW THAT money had exchanged hands on the day that now seemed so long ago, she preferred to think she had been taken by force and that her parents had not had anything to do with it. Far better to be stolen than handed over.

"You don't understand. He was a priest!" Arrosa exclaimed. "We were so poor at the time that we made soup of boiled roots, and he promised to provide a good home for you, where you would be fed and nurtured. He promised . . ."

Gotzone listened but found herself thinking of another, who had clung to his memories of a son through a lifetime in prison, and who'd been prepared to walk all the way home from Toulouse, even though he could hardly stand. She choked, but not at the story her mother told. She was thinking of one who had treated her with kindness, and who deserved so much more than the dishonesty and surliness she had shown him in return.

"... your father ..." Arrosa was saying.

"*Aita?*" Gotzone said, suddenly alert.

"He took it very hard," Arrosa confided, as if a man's second thoughts were more than enough to absolve him of recrimination for an abhorrent deed. "You have no idea." Arrosa shook her head at the memory of it. "He wandered around the village looking for you. He was heartbroken and I couldn't talk to him. No one could ..."

"He missed me?" Gotzone asked.

"Oh, yes," Arrosa said.

But the woman's eyes gave her away, and Gotzone didn't believe her.

Arrosa made a fire in the hearth. As the flames caught, she fed tinder and kindling until the orange tongues licked hungrily. Then she went to the bedroom and came back with Gotzone's discarded clothes. Resolutely, she tossed them onto the burning wood.

"What are you doing?" Gotzone cried, dashing to the hearth. But the pants and tunic already smoldered. Black smoke wreathed around them as the fabric darkened and then burst into flame. "What have you done?"

"It's for your own good," Arrosa said, and Gotzone knew she was right, for it was a sin for a girl to dress as a boy. *La Pucelle d'Orléans* had paid the price at the stake, as many now knew, for stories like that spread like flames in dry grass. But the clothes that now burned had enabled Gotzone to pass freely in a hostile world. Without them, she felt trapped in her mother's dress.

"Come—it's time to prepare for the evening meal," Arrosa said. "Your father will be home soon. And your brothers. You must be careful of them."

"Will they know who I am?" Gotzone asked.

Arrosa hesitated. "You can make the bread and I will tell your father how helpful you were," she finally replied, and again Gotzone saw the truth in her eyes. She saw how very worried her mother was.

◆　◆　◆

GOTZONE HAD NEVER MADE BREAD before. Arrosa gave her an apron to wear and before long the apron was white with flour. Gotzone's hands were caked with dough. She had to scrape the dough off and add it to the lump she was kneading, and still she felt as if she wore gloves. When her father came home, he just stared at her. Arrosa explained to him that Gotzone had just come for a visit, and he glared at her suspiciously.

"You can never trust a churchman," he spat, darkly, as if the mark of the priest were still on her and she shared in his duplicity.

During the meal, he continued to stare. By then, Gotzone's two brothers had come in and sat elbow to elbow at the table. They slid their eyes at their father and then turned them on her, and she could feel the thoughts worming through their heads. Having pretended to be a boy herself, she could almost imagine what they were thinking.

"I didn't know we had *two* sisters," said the oldest, whom she remembered as a baby and who was now about seven. His mean little eyes shifted toward the little girl that sat on her mother's knee, then back to Gotzone, the heat of a wild animal radiating from his challenging gaze. Their father cuffed him and he wailed. Under the table, the boy kicked Gotzone in the shin. She winced but didn't cry out, and the boy's face twisted into a sly grin. The younger brother had a plump, happy face. Gotzone immediately liked him and gave him an extra piece of her bread. When the older brother saw this, he pouted and made a grab for it, but their father cuffed him again.

Halfway through the meal, with some of the soup still left in the communal bowl and bread still on the table, the man got up and stomped out of the house. Everyone huddled in silence until Arrosa, too, rose, and Gotzone helped her clean up. She was almost as tall as her mother and the two of them worked side by side.

"Why did you tell Aita I was just visiting?" Gotzone wanted to know.

"You've been gone a long time and there is much you don't understand," Arrosa said, her voice low.

"But I'm not just visiting—this is my home."

"You are not safe here," her mother said.

◆　◆　◆

GOTZONE DIDN'T SLEEP THAT FIRST night. Each pop of a dying ember in the hearth, every rustle of a mouse questing for crumbs, made her start and spasm, thinking they might be the sounds of a man creeping up on the pallet where she lay in a corner of the main room. She had no reason to think her father was that way, and her brothers weren't old enough, but they were all males and that was the problem. Young as she was, she knew far too much about men and feared the worst.

In the gray dawn, she felt a presence and opened her eyes to find her father towering over her. She didn't have to see his expression to feel the unhappiness and indecision that radiated from his shadowy form. Choked with alarm, she lay still, and he finally turned and left the house. Later, her mother crouched in front of the hearth, poking at an iron pot with her spoon. The brothers still snored. Gotzone closed her eyes and when she opened them again, her little sister sat on the floor next to her, huddled there in somber silence. The girl was beautiful, with dark wavy hair and dark lashes, smooth milky skin. Her eyes captured some of the firelight from the hearth. On impulse, Gotzone opened the blanket and the little girl crept in next to her. The warmth of the little body comforted her. The silky hair filled Gotzone with dreams of her own childhood, or rather a childhood that she might have had under different circumstances. Because those memories were gone. Aside from bits and flashes, she could hardly recall what her life had been like before the priest spirited her away.

Gotzone knew she was tainted. The priest had had a presence that lingered like a foul odor that made her mother shrink from her. Careful not to disturb her sister, who now slumbered peacefully, Gotzone got out of bed, slipped off the nightclothes that Arrosa had given her, and quickly pulled on the only dress she now had.

Arrosa looked harried, as she hovered in the small house.

"What do you expect a man like your father to do?" she finally blurted. Her eyes darted toward the door of the house, which her husband had slammed behind him, earlier in the morning. "Is he supposed to find a husband for you as if you never left? Who would want you?" Arrosa shook her head. "You know what people will think of you. You know what they will say and what they might do. You must know the position this puts us in."

Gotzone shuddered. "I don't want to get married." She tried to convince herself she was too young, but she knew it wasn't true. Some girls wed even before they started to bleed, and many wed soon after.

Arrosa placed her hands over her ears, recoiling and shaking her head. She shrank away, but Gotzone pressed her case.

"I don't expect anything of Aita," she said. "I can't change the past and neither can you, and I don't expect things to be the way they were. I can't even remember ... *before*." She was crying now. "How can I expect you to accept me when I can't even accept myself?"

Arrosa softened. She couldn't quite embrace her daughter, who had died to her and come back a stranger. There was too much guilt and remorse, and now too much unpredictability. But Arrosa was not made of stone.

"I will talk to your father," she said.

"No ... no ..." Gotzone murmured, not wanting to pit a wife against her husband.

"I can't make any promises. But I will see what I can do," Arrosa said, resolutely, reaching out and daring to touch the girl at last.

◆　◆　◆

THE FAMILY HAD SIX CHICKENS, and Gotzone heard their frenzied squawks as her brother chased them around the yard. Once the plaintive cries of a captured bird had quieted, Gotzone's father went out with his slaughtering blade in hand. The silence became one of those meaningful voids that a sensitive soul could sink into and forget about other things. In due time, Arrosa plucked the fowl and clawed out its insides. She hung it on a hook in a corner of the house while she swept the floor and straightened up the furnishings, and Gotzone watched with the same helplessness the chicken must have felt in its final moments. Things were happening much too quickly. The carcass was oiled and seasoned and placed in a lidded pot on the hearth, and her mother was chopping vegetables. Gotzone's little sister sat on the floor and watched. Soon she would be old enough to go to the well and draw water for the family, as Gotzone had once done.

Then, as the savory aroma of roasting bird filled the house, an old man appeared at the door. The top of his head was bald, with a rim of wiry gray hair that feathered over his ears. The lines and wrinkles in his skin looked like animal tracks that had dried and cracked in mud, and his beard flared down against his chest. The single chicken would not have made much of a meal for the whole family and their guest, but it was enough for the men, and Gotzone hung back with her mother and sister, watching the men and boys dip their fingers into the bowl. The old man chewed with his mouth open, his eyes drifting over to dwell appraisingly on Gotzone.

The old man had many sheep and was considered to be rich. But his three previous wives had all died, leaving him alone. Gotzone was skinny as a boy, he pointed out, and was that the only dress she had, he wanted to know, perhaps wondering how expensive it would be to clothe her? Did she know how to cook and had she ever shorn a sheep? Gotzone's heart hammered. She kept her eyes on the floor in front of her.

After the meal, Arrosa gave her daughter the task of serving tea, and the old man leaned forward as she placed his cup in front of him. His nostrils flared. Gotzone trembled as the deal was struck. Her face burned and her stomach knotted. Placing a hand to her abdomen, she rushed from the house and leaned against the outer wall to vomit.

◆　◆　◆

GOTZONE LAY ON HER SIDE with her knees pulled up to her chest and the blanket over her head. She didn't remember having slept, but the dream was real enough. She'd dreamed she was outside in the hard-swept yard, playing a game with her little sister, shaking pebbles in her hand and then casting them on the ground, when a cloud came over the sun—a dark cloud with a bruised, puckered face like that of a man who'd been in a fight. In the dream, her father came out of the house with his slaughtering knife, and he walked up to her and knelt by her side. Patting her head, he gently stroked her hair. His eyes were soft. They seemed to pity her. Too late she saw the knife start to move.

"Come on now and get yourself up," Arrosa said, a little out of breath. She had dragged a heavy metal tub to the center of the room. "You don't know how lucky you are that your father found such an agreeable man to husband you. The younger men laughed in your father's face! But Abarran is old enough to overlook certain things. At his age, he is willing to forget . . ."

Gotzone didn't respond.

"Come now and stop feeling sorry for yourself. Abarran said he would be by to collect you today, and we have to get you washed and properly dressed. We have to get you ready." Arrosa reached under the table for the water buckets. A tender look crept into her eyes. "I will give you another dress—the best one I have," she said, softly.

But Gotzone had made up her mind. She threw aside her blanket and got up from the pallet. Looking at her mother, her heart broke. "Ama, I'm sorry. Please thank Aita for me and tell him how sorry I am," she said, suddenly embracing Arrosa, who stiffened like the trunk of a tree.

"What are you doing?"

"I have to leave," Gotzone said.

"What do you mean? Where are you going?"

But Gotzone had already turned her shoulder, wiping the back of a hand against her eyes. At the door, she paused long enough to give Arrosa one last, lingering look, trying to preserve the image that would last forever—that of the stooped figure with the wizened face, eyes that already had the sad, desperate look of dawning awareness.

"Goodbye, Ama," Gotzone said, huskily, her vision blurring, her heart hammering and aching, as she turned away for the final time and fled the house.

She was nothing if not resolute, for that was the kind of soul she had become—hardened by what life had offered her and unyielding in her response. She had never been to Abarran's house but knew he had a lambing shed and there was only one house in the village with one. She saw him in the back, collecting firewood from the pile next to the shed, and remained hidden until he returned inside. She crept to his front door, which was already warming in the eastern sun, and placed the pair of silver candlesticks on the step. Then, she turned and hurried away.

When she reached the fateful well, she faltered, with the full weight of what she was about to do crushing down on her. With the priest, she had at least had a home, and then, on the road with Jean-Pierre, she had had a purpose, of sorts—even if it was just to keep an eye on an old man and aid in his doddering progress.

Now, however, her illusions were like wild birds she had released from a wicker cage. Once the well was behind her, she breathed easier. But as a young woman alone, with truly nowhere to go and without the protection of her family, she had little hope. She could only put one foot in front of the other, praying that the Virgin was not so cold as she had every right to be, that she would overlook a fallen girl's sinful nature and open her arms at last.

All too soon, she sat on a rock along the pilgrim's road, faint from hunger and exhaustion. Her body jerked and spasmed with the creeping cold of the coming night. With her arms crossed over her stomach, she sat with her knees together and her head hanging down, taking the only pleasure she could in the moment, which was thinking of Abarran's reaction when he found the candlesticks.

She wondered if he would think it some cruel trick. He might suspect Gotzone was somehow behind the unexpected gifts, for he was a crafty old man and surely knew that rain seldom falls from a clear sky. He might wonder how someone like she might have come by such treasures. But it wouldn't keep him from snatching them up and secreting them in his house, she was sure. Perhaps he would consider the candlesticks a fair trade for the marriage he now would not have.

But fatigue got the best of her, and her mind started to drift. Arranged marriages happened all the time, and if the priest had never entered her life, perhaps she would have gone through with it. Certainly, many a young woman had married a man far older, for whatever reason. But Gotzone could not abide the thought of marriage to anyone, let alone that wrinkled old man. She would rather be exactly where she was, sitting by the roadside with dusk falling, with the stars coming out and the cooling air stealing her breath and carrying it away in disappearing clouds.

———•———

Magdalena Laux Kraymer, as she was now known, had long dreamed of finding a kindred soul—someone more like her than not—somewhere in this world. She could almost feel a presence, the way one senses a spring rain in the offing. But along with rain comes the chance of a storm, and Magdalena's heightened perceptions hinted at other things as well. She saw visions of a candle that flickered in darkness and an unfilled grave, and naturally assumed they had something to do with the political career to which her husband aspired.

She slipped out of her bedroom in the Penn's Woods château that she called home and made her way to the room where her husband slept.

"Mr. Kraymer, it's time to rise," she said, entering after a brief knock. She went to the window and thrust the drapes open. Sunlight poured in and Lawrence groaned loudly, squinting and raising an arm to shield his face.

"Come on, now," Magdalena chided, affably. " It's already late and you know they will be waiting for you at Hugo's Tavern. I tried to tell you not to schedule the event so early. It was you who wanted to get it over and done with so you could move on to the next town by suppertime."

Lawrence groaned again. He often complained that electors were a funny lot. It would have been unethical to pay for their votes, but they wouldn't mind listening to his pitch at the tavern as long as their tankards were topped and they weren't footing the bill.

"You're the one who wanted to be in the assembly," Magdalena reminded him.

"I know," he relented, sighing. Swinging his legs past the edge of the bed, he sat up, pulling the blanket with him so that it bunched up around his waist. Magdalena turned her back while he switched out of his bedclothes. She listened as he pulled on his trousers and heard the rattle of his belt buckle.

"Are you decent?" she asked.

"Almost," he grumbled, and she had to fight the grin that tugged and pulled. Lawrence could be a handful at times, especially when forced to do something that he didn't want to do, such as rise with the sun and campaign in the surrounding countryside. But a little inconvenience was a small price to pay for a voice in matters that not only affected him, with his sawmills and drayage company, but others as well, all the way down to a farmer on his land.

For breakfast, Magdalena ate a slice of buttered toast, while Lawrence had his three eggs and a slice of ham. Coffee made the meal a little more special than usual. The roasted beans weren't as readily available as the more commonplace teas, but Lawrence had developed a taste for it, especially with cream.

Lawrence helped with the dishes, and she watched him from the corner of her eye, feeling the warmth of his companionship. The meeting at Hugo's would take place at noon, due to Lawrence's concern that if it were held much later, the electors would have imbibed too much and lost focus. His goal was to make his pitch and then leave before things got too rowdy. By the time they stood on the cobbled street before the tavern door, boisterous voices indeed issued forth, and Magdalena was only too glad to take her husband's arm and offer what support she could.

The public house was dark and gloomy. A fire crackled in the hearth, despite the summer weather, making the room stuffy and overly warm. About fifteen men lounged at the counter or sat at the small cluster of tables. But what caught Magdalena's attention right away was a smell not associated with the cooking fire or the men wearing justaucorps, which were long-sleeved, knee-length jackets. Smoke was a thing so commonplace in the colony that it usually didn't bear mention. Land clearing, refuse burning, and food preparation, not to mention the warming fires of early mornings, created a haze that clung to clothes. But the kind of smoke that Magdalena now smelled was different. It was bitter and rancid—a stench that crawled up the nose and soured in the throat—and glancing toward the back of the room, she saw them. Pennsylvania backwoodsmen. Sharp-eyed, with bearded faces and scratchy necks. These were men from the backcountry, where they lived in log hovels and shot wild game for food—deer when they could get them, the occasional turkey, but often as not, squirrels and rabbits and anything else that moved. The settlements were few in the rough country known as the Appalachians, and these men lived even farther out, where the constant fear of Indian attack was as real as breathing.

She could sense the effort it took for Lawrence to steel himself. Whereas any man could become quarrelsome, especially with a few tankards in him, the backwoodsmen were often wilder than the aborigines themselves and were bound to be unpredictable. Some of them had traveled over a hundred miles and still wore their dirty deerskin hunting shirts and filthy linen pants. These were men who probably couldn't vote, anyway, and in a fit of pique, she wondered why they had not just holed up in their hills and tippled the homemade spirits they were famous for.

No doubt caught up in his thoughts, Lawrence seated her at one of the empty tables. Most respectable women avoided such establishments, and the men eyed Magdalena warily, taking note of what to report back to their wives. Most of the townsfolk and even those on the surrounding farms knew of Magdalena Kraymer by now. They had known her when she was a child with red hair like a campfire, and they knew her now as the strong-willed if not outright difficult woman of Lawrence's castle.

Standing to make his pitch, Lawrence launched into how increasingly unfair the British Parliament had become, requiring that English ships trade only with England or one of its American or West Indies colonies, in spite of higher offers from other quarters. What did a legislative body an ocean away know about life in the colonies, he asked. Perhaps Londoners knew of crops that could be wiped out by too little rain—or too much—but what did they know of the voracious vermin of a looming forest that could eat a crop to the ground? And who were they to decide with whom Pennsylvania colonists could trade, given the multitudes of uncertainties and the importance of getting your due when it came to putting food on the table, not to mention survival itself?

"Hear! Hear!" one man and then another shouted. But the backwoodsmen just glared. They were subsistence farmers at best and had not come to argue about something as meaningless to them as the prices of timber or wheat.

"What about dem savages what plagues us?" one of the backwoodsmen shouted.

"We haven't had an Indian attack in twenty years," one of the locals said, and several others murmured agreement.

"Well, that's you, innit—livin' here all cozy-like?" the back-woodsman snarled and one of his associates howled like a wolf. "You live out there in Indian country an' yer scalp makes a loose-fittin' cap, I'll tell you that an' make it plain." He leveled his gaze on Lawrence. "What's yer fancy 'sembly gonna do about the womens and chil'ren what needs defendin'?"

Lawrence looked a little rattled. Magdalena well knew how the people in the backwoods clamored day and night for protection. Having moved beyond the creeping pale of civilization, they demanded that a militia secure their homes. Some even called for a provincial army, and it galled them that the Quaker assembly was slow to act. The Quakers claimed moral objection to any kind of war effort, and Lawrence had gone to great lengths to give the Quakers their due—up to a point. But he was always quick to point out that he wasn't blind, and held the firm opinion that money was at the heart of the problem, as usual. Militia were more inclined to protect their own than go too far afield. And provincials had to be paid. They had to be clothed and if they didn't already have the muskets they hunted with, they needed to be armed as well. Not many in the assembly had the stomach to foot such a bill for a smattering of settlers who had no business placing themselves in harm's way in the first place.

"I'll see what I can do," he said.

"He'll see what 'ee can do," the backwoodsman sneered, turning to his fellows. "Him that already coddles with the heathen and keeps one of 'em on that very property o' his." It was a well-known fact that a Lenape named John lived in a cabin on Lawrence's estate.

"Isn't the fighting over by now?" one of the locals asked in an apparent effort to help Lawrence out. The frontier skirmishes seemed to have quieted down since the end of Queen Anne's War.

In fairness, however, it should be said that in the backcountry, where news traveled slowly, battles were often fought long after an armistice was reached.

"You kin come an' pay me a visit an' see for yerself," the woodsman spat, to the approval of those in his camp.

Lawrence attempted to move to safer ground. With perspiration now pouring down his neck and soaking the collar of his shirt, he talked about the need to improve the roads so that goods could be transported quickly and safely. Improvised bridges made of logs laid down crosswise through swampy areas had to be reinforced, and real bridges needed to be built at streams where fords still existed.

But the men in the tavern were losing interest. Some wandered outside to "water the oak," and one of the backwoodsmen circled behind Magdalena's table. At first, she ignored the malevolent presence, but then he bent down to take a sniff at her. She rounded upon him with a withering look, and he backed away, sneering.

By the time an incensed Lawrence got to the table, the backwoodsman had already returned to his fellows.

"What was that all about?" Lawrence demanded, craning his neck to keep an eye on the man who had paid his wife such unwanted attention.

"It's nothing, dear," Magdalena said. "If you're here to join me, then do so and take a seat."

"What did he have to say for himself? Tell me!" Lawrence insisted, still standing.

"I can take care of myself," Magdalena assured him, looking up at him with a quick, tight smile.

"So you say," he retorted, still hot under the collar.

"I can't talk to you if you're going to loom over me like that."

He glared at her, then sighed and lowered himself to the edge of a chair.

"Thank you." Magdalena placed a hand on his and gave a little squeeze. "If you're going to be in the assembly, I will be alone most of the time. We talked about this and you know it to be true. We have to figure this out."

Lawrence shot a glance toward the cluster of backwoodsmen. He generally didn't hold onto his anger for very long and already seemed to be calming down. But he appeared to have lost his enthusiasm for oratory. He rubbed a finger against his forehead, perhaps remembering what had happened to his first wife and fearing for his second. Perhaps even doubting his choice to run for office in the first place if it meant having to live so far away from Magdalena.

"I'm fine, believe me," she said.

"I don't know," Lawrence responded, moodily. "Maybe we should just go home."

"Didn't you want to stop at some other places and work on the votes you need?"

"Some other time, maybe. Let's just get out of here. I should go see John, anyway."

"Don't worry about him."

"I have to warn him that some folks might have it in for him."

Magdalena leaned close, so that only Lawrence could hear.

"Do you think he doesn't already know that?" she asked.

He gave her a hard look, then nodded, grudgingly. John was the sole survivor of his entire village. First the smallpox and measles had decimated his people, then white vigilantes did their part. Lawrence did what he could for his friend, giving him a place to live in a remote corner of the estate, where he could have all the privacy he needed. But John spent a lot of time in the deep woods and the forest could swallow a man. He could be gone for days or weeks or even months at a time, and Lawrence never knew if and when he would ever see him again.

◆　◆　◆

With Lawrence now in the assembly, Magdalena grew used to being alone. She spent her mornings out of doors, weeding the garden, feeding the chickens, or going for a walk if no other task pressed. In the afternoons, she liked to make a pot of tea and read by the hearth in the sitting room. Preparing supper always took a fair amount of time, especially for one who didn't quite share the culinary talents of her mother and older sister. Then, after visiting with her husband—on those increasingly rare occasions when he was home—she retired to her bedchamber for the night.

Lately, though, she was on edge. Her nights made her uneasy, for they were inky and far too deep. Wooden beams popped and cracked for no apparent reason, and there were other sounds that she could not identify. A mouse, perhaps, or curtains that stirred as if brushed by a hand. Magdalena wasn't afraid of ghosts, if indeed they existed, but the darkness unnerved her. Even as a child, she would crawl under the covers to the bottom of the bed and hold her breath until dawn. Lawrence had offered that she sleep in the same bed with him. But she didn't see this as a good solution for a Cathar woman in a chaste marriage. It was just asking for trouble, as far as she was concerned.

Inevitably, the dreams came. She was in an empty space filled with the smell of damp rock. At first, the darkness seemed so complete she couldn't see her hand in front of her face. Then she saw the flicker of a candle. Holding her hands out and moving toward it, she tripped and fell and the ground opened up. She was in some kind of hole. It was too deep to climb out of and she tried to calm her hammering heart, attempting to quell the scream that rose on her tongue.

She woke in her bed, drenched with sweat.

"Who's there?" she said, into the dark.

A wind had come up in the night and a shutter banged against the side of the house. A fox barked. An owl hooted. Something made a thin, plaintive cry. Magdalena's throat tightened, and she felt as if a sock had been stuffed in her mouth and that she had to draw breath through it to stay alive.

"Who are you?" she demanded.

There was no response and she began to tremble. Her breathing turned ragged. So terribly alone in a room by herself in the middle of a black night on the edge of the wilderness. Her hands shook as she lit the lamp by the bedside. The chamber bloomed with light.

"Where are you?" she breathed, unconvinced that no one was there.

When Jean-Pierre got out of prison, the world that awaited him was strange beyond measure. Sunlight felt like broken glass in his eyes, and people were like phantoms that came and went, much as the specters that had filled his dreams for so many years. The commis de police in Toulouse was a maddening fly that wouldn't leave him alone, and the other one—that Gaspar or whatever the commis called him—was just as bad. Wherever Jean-Pierre turned, one or the other of them seemed stuck in his face. Only one thing mattered, and as far as he could see, neither of these men had anything to do with it.

Then there was the boy, who seemed to appear out of nowhere and wouldn't leave. Jean-Pierre didn't begrudge his presence, for he seemed of no consequence. In truth, Jean-Pierre half-expected him to grow wings and flap off, like so many of the creatures of what, to him, had seemed an endless night. Sometimes, Jean-Pierre even forgot the boy was there with him. He would thrust his staff at the ground and struggle forward, seeing only the road ahead and an endless horizon that teased and beckoned. Then, he would hear something or think a thought and turn and lo and behold, there the lad was, tagging along, maybe whistling like a bird or tossing stones into the bushes or whatever it was that waifs did when they didn't know what to do with themselves.

Most of the time, Jean-Pierre ignored him, though the incident with the hare gave him pause. The boy had made a good throw, though he looked a bit awkward doing it. Jean-Pierre couldn't help but think that his own son, Pierre, would have taken pride in such a well-placed shot and the prospects of a fine meal that it afforded. But the boy, who called himself Gabriel, seemed crestfallen. It simply didn't make any sense to Jean-Pierre.

Nor did it make sense the way his own heart melted at Gabriel's plight. There was much more at stake than the tears of a boy, he was inclined to remind himself. The world that Jean-Pierre knew had broken into pieces, and an old man who didn't recognize himself waded through fragments that seemed to dash and dart around him like a school of minnows. What did a *garçon* and whatever thoughts he had matter, one way or another? What was a dead hare that it had to be cried over? What was a Gypsy woman who showed up in her caravan and who acted like she was the one to make decisions, when nothing at all mattered but the vision that had both inspired and tormented a prisoner who had just about given up hope that he would ever see the blue sky again?

Jean-Pierre understood pain, first of the heart and then, as a result of his unexpected freedom, of a body that failed and failed and then failed again. Even he knew that he would never have survived the journey to his destination if the Gypsy woman had not offered him a ride. And then there was the boy, always present when Jean-Pierre needed him, saving him from arrest by the soldiers from Toulouse, offering him what little food the lad had, and then sticking by him, always there, right there, when most would have walked on. The awful woods where his men had been ambushed were hard to bear, and seeing that gloomy patch nearly broke him all over again. The thunder of the musket fire deafened him anew, as it had over the many years, in the dark of the night and in the night of the day, before the scholar brought a proper bed and a lamp, and even then, when the lamplight burned and Jean-Pierre watched the oil dwindle and knew what must come next. The sound of the muskets made him jolt and quiver, and there was the boy again, slipping his hand into Jean-Pierre's and lending an unimaginable strength to a man who would have otherwise fallen to his knees and yielded to the moldering loam.

Jean-Pierre didn't understand what Gabriel meant to him, not yet—not then, not when he still hoped against hope that his manoir remained intact, and that he had a wife and child who still waited at the open door, unscathed and unaltered by time. All he could think of was the dream that he had lived in and a reality that now threatened to crush the life out of him. The overgrown estate and the boarded-up manoir, the emptiness that waited inside. The dresser with the cracked mirror made him wish that he had died in his cell. Better to have perished than to be assaulted by a terrible truth.

Once again, Gabriel came to his rescue, bringing the villagers with their food and medicines, the trunks of clothing and furnishings they had stolen, and Jean-Pierre cursed them. He didn't want to blame them for taking what they had from the manoir, back when they thought their seigneur was dead—but the other thing, the worse thing, was more than he could bear. A fire smoldered, for they had not only helped themselves to his possessions, they now deprived him of news of his wife and son. Jean-Pierre went from door to door in the village, and it was always the same. The terrified villagers claimed the absolution of ignorance. The soldiers were the ones who'd drunk the seigneur's wine and soiled his bed linen with their filthy bodies, the villagers said. The soldiers were the ones who had moved into the house the seigneur had left behind, and how was a villager to know what went on within those fortified walls and what had become of the seigneur's family?

They pleaded that they were not to blame. But blame them Jean-Pierre did, and now that Gabriel was gone, he blamed them for this, too. François tried to reason with him, pointing out that Jean-Pierre was alive and that where there was life, there was hope, and one could say that François should know. François would not even have been born without such hope. Against the odds, his father, Guy Aguirre, had, in fact, survived the ambush in the woods. A peasant driving a wooden cart found him still breathing and took him to the peasant's home, where he nursed the stricken man for several months. When Guy returned to his village, it was with an arm that hung uselessly at his side. He had to walk with a crutch. But he was alive and well enough to father a son, before finally succumbing to his wounds.

François had never known Guy the way that Jean-Pierre had, as a vigorous and vital man who was far better with the sword than most and whose only flaw was a mortal vulnerability to musket balls that would have felled an ox. The father François had known was hardly the shadow of this man.

"You know that he loved you," François said, as they stood in the dappled shade of the locust tree that overlooked Guy's grave. Behind them was the simple cottage where François lived, alone. "He never gave up hope. We didn't have much money, but he didn't hesitate to spend every penny of it on anyone who was willing to look for you and your family. He sent agents to Toulouse and everywhere else and even sought information from the king's court in Versailles, all to no avail. You disappeared without a trace. The king's soldiers moved into the manoir and then Madame Eleanor disappeared, along with Pierre. By the time my father was well enough to return home, after being shot, the manoir was empty. Everyone and every-thing was gone."

"Guy was a better man than I ever was," Jean-Pierre said, mean-ing every word.

"He said the same thing about you," François observed. "You probably don't remember my mother, but she was Madame Elea-nor's servant."

Jean-Pierre frowned.

"She also did scullery," François prompted.

"Hannah?" Jean-Pierre said, his voice leaking out of him. How could he have forgotten a young girl so sweet of face and light of foot? His heart ached.

"She said working for you and Madame Eleanor were the best years of her life."

Jean-Pierre looked down at the grave beside Guy's, and it seemed too much. Too much gone. Too much taken. His sorrow hardened and his rage once again bubbled. His hands flexed into fists, and it took every bit of effort he could muster to keep them at his sides, when he wanted to raise them up and shake them at the sky.

◆　◆　◆

WITH THE FATE OF HIS wife and son unknown, and without the slightest idea of where to seek them out, when Guy Aguirre had already made inquiries throughout the land, Jean-Pierre entered a very dark place. Villagers still showed up at his door with this or that, items they wished to return to him now that he was back in the manoir. But this flow had slowed to a trickle, and Jean-Pierre knew there was plenty more still out there. In the absence of Eleanor and Pierre, he coveted anything they might have gazed upon or touched, and which still might bear the lingering essence of their presence. In their absence, such things were all he had left, and he paced the manoir irritably, wondering what kept François. Then, when he finally sat next to the youth on the bench of the wagon, he didn't understand why François drove so slowly. Each bump and jolt of the conveyance sent ripples of rage through him.

"We're almost there, sir," François said, lifting his chin toward a stone farmhouse tucked into the side of the hill, surrounded by a grove of walnut trees. Jean-Pierre's eyes itched. Rumor had it that the farmer owned things he could never have afforded in a million years, and Jean-Pierre's fingers twitched. His jaws tightened.

By the time François set the brake, Jean-Pierre was already striding toward the isolated home. When no one answered his furious pounding on the door, he stepped back. A helpless despair piled up in his throat, and he gestured for François to force the door with his shoulder.

Entering the house was like stepping into a cave. The windows were shuttered, making the room seem cluttered, as if gloominess had a presence all its own that could gather and collect and stand its ground. The old and slightly rancid smell of cooked onions pinched his nose. Like many of the homes in the region, there was an attached barn that added the sharp odor of manure, and a woman stood just inside the connecting door. Upon hearing Jean-Pierre's ferocious knocking, she must have fled to the barn for a pitchfork, which she now held in readiness, her eyes wild with fear.

Dismissing her as a threat, Jean-Pierre motioned for François to search the house, which the youth set about doing. In one corner, he flipped the lid of a wooden chest that sat atop a small table. Rummaging through it, he took out a cloth bundle and placed it on the table. He unwrapped the bundle and grunted, then, with a triumphant gaze, held up a silver fork for the seigneur to see. The bundle held several other utensils of similar value.

But Jean-Pierre was staring at a rug that lay on the floor in front of the cooking hearth. The rug had a dark, circular pattern that would have appeared red under better lighting.

"Where did that come from?" he demanded of the woman, gesturing toward the rug. His eyes narrowed with indignation.

"My husband give that to me," the woman said, her knuckles whitening on the handle of the pitchfork.

"Your husband gave you a Turkish rug that has been in my family since the Crusades?" Jean-Pierre said, barely containing his rage. "Just like he gave you the silver forks and spoons? What else did this husband of yours give you?"

"He give them to me, that's all." The woman's voice broke. "He said they were nobody's anymore and that I should have them. He said they were mine to keep!"

"Where is he, that I might speak with him?" Jean-Pierre said, icily.

"He's nearby—I don't know," the woman cried. "I don't know what you want with him!"

"What I *want*?"

Jean-Pierre's eyes felt like fireballs. He gestured toward the carpet, and François rolled it up, tucked it under his arm, and then, after a quick glance at the seigneur, carried it out to the wagon. Jean-Pierre smoldered as he, himself, snatched up the silverware. Truly, if this were a different time, when seigneurs were less accountable for their actions, he might have waited for the farmer's return and had him hanged from one of the trees outside.

"You will tell your husband he is lucky that he wasn't here," Jean-Pierre said, in a tone that left no doubt as to the state he was in. "Tell him to pay me a visit so that we can discuss what he owes me. You tell him that, hear?"

"What he owes you?" the woman said, still holding the pitchfork as she followed Jean-Pierre to the door.

But having made his wishes known, Jean-Pierre now ignored her, ducking his head as he left the farmhouse.

"Somewhere else you would like to go?" François asked.

Jean-Pierre shook his head sullenly.

"Let's just go home," he muttered.

For once the cool outside air bathed his face and his heat subsided, he felt sick to his stomach. He was disgusted with himself for his comportment in the farmhouse and for what he might have done had the farmer been present. Over and over, he asked himself what he had tried to accomplish. A silver spoon was not the hand that had held it, and a carpet was not the slippered foot that had once graced the pile. Eleanor, herself, would have pointed out that despair was no excuse for becoming a monster.

Back at the manoir, he called out for Maude, a villager who had become his housekeeper, but she didn't respond. The manoir seemed as uneasy with him as he was with himself, and he went to the kitchen. He didn't know the contents of his own kitchen and had to search through cupboards and drawers until he finally found the bottle of brandy. He took it to the sitting room, where he sat in front of the unlit fireplace and stared at the previous night's ashes. He had forgotten a glass but shrugged this off, uncorking the bottle and raising it to his lips. The bottle was soon empty, and he had half a mind to go and look for another. But by then he felt as if a wooly sheep had bedded down in his head, and he didn't hear the sound of the empty bottle as it slipped from his fingers to bounce and roll on the floor.

◆ ◆ ◆

Jean-Pierre awakened to a loud pounding noise. He still sat in the sitting room, and from the dampness and odor of his clothes, he realized he must have spent the night in the chair. The window drapes were still wide open from the day before, and his boots lay in the middle of the floor. Staggering to his feet, he kicked the empty brandy bottle out of his way and headed for the foyer. He yanked the door open and raised a hand to shield his face from the bright morning sun.

Three women stood on the threshold. The foremost one had short dark hair that looked as if she had combed it with her fingers, and a snug cuirass over a knee-length tunic. Sharp eyes sized him up, and her mouth was set in a firm line of disapproval. Behind her, the other two were similarly dressed, with pistols in their belts.

"My mistress bids you hello and good health," she said, without introduction, as if expecting him to know full well who she and her mistress were. She stared past him into the interior of the house.

Jean-Pierre recoiled. Female soldiers were rare in a land that largely subscribed to a patriarchal system of rule strongly rooted in Roman Christianity. The only person Jean-Pierre could think of who might contravene this tendency—along with other rules of accepted behavior—was his sister-in-law, Esclarmonde, and he had not seen her since his marriage to Eleanor. Esclarmonde had strong ideas about how she and her sister should have lived, and none of them included marrying a southern nobleman. The subsequent birth of Pierre made matters worse. To Esclarmonde, it was an indication of just how far Eleanor had fallen from the virtues of the True Way.

"We have heard of your return, and my mistress wonders why you have not yet called upon her."

Why indeed? Jean-Pierre thought, irritably. It had never occurred to him to get in touch with a woman who had treated him so dismissively. As far as he was concerned, it would have been like sticking his hand into a box known to contain a venomous snake.

"She said to tell you she has information you will want to hear," the woman went on, and Jean-Pierre's eyes widened at the thought that Esclarmonde might have heard of his disappearance. She would have known of the Dragonnades, just like any other noble in the southland, and it would have been just like her to come to her sister's rescue, if only to gloat about it afterward.

His gaze shifted to the carriage that waited in the yard, as his thoughts now reached a feverish pitch. Relief flooded him at the prospect that Eleanor was safely ensconced in a fortress that had once withstood medieval sieges. He cursed himself for not thinking of Esclarmonde in the first place.

A short time later, he sat in the carriage as it rolled along. The female soldier, whom he now knew as Claire, sat across from him, watching him like a hawk that observed the movements of a mouse in the grass. Perhaps she was amused. It was hard to tell.

"You don't much like me, do you?" she said.

Jean-Pierre raised his eyebrows.

"Why would I not like you?"

"You think a woman like me doesn't know her place," Claire sniffed. "You think we should be cooking food and having babies, while men like you decide what to do with us."

When he didn't respond, Claire leaned back against her seat, regarding him with brooding, lidded eyes. Her face twitched, and he began to wonder if her attitude was an indication of what he might expect from Esclarmonde. Not that it mattered what Esclarmonde thought, he mused, as long as Eleanor was safe and sound.

"I will fetch my wife back home and trouble you no more," he offered.

Surprise rippled across Claire's face. She opened her mouth as if to say something, then clamped it shut again, turning her head to the side. As bold as she had been earlier, she now retreated into a silence that should have concerned him. But peace could be deceptive when it obscured a truth, and for the moment, at least, he was relieved that the uncouth woman left him alone as the carriage trundled along.

Twilight had begun to gather, slipping darkly from tree to tree and finally drawing a curtain across the road. A stiff wind came up, the kind of blustery pushing and shoving that meant a change was on the way. A smattering of large drops hit the carriage. Thunder grumbled. The conveyance rocked from side to side, and Jean-Pierre was relieved to see a lighted window at last, shining like a staring eye in the gathering night.

Climbing stiffly from the coach, he drew his cloak around him and turned his collar up. He didn't have to knock, as the heavy wooden door of the castle keep had already opened. An old woman crouched with a lantern in her hand, and Jean-Pierre's chest tightened.

"Marie!" he gasped, as if the name were an oath. He remembered her as the housekeeper who never let Esclarmonde out of her sight.

The old woman held the lantern aloft, eyeing him critically.

"Well, look at you!" she commented.

"I might have changed a bit," he allowed.

"Changed? More like death couldn't swallow you and had to spit you back out!" She gave her head a shake and muttered to herself, then she bade him enter. Pausing long enough to blow out the lantern, she hung it on a hook, then turned and cast a final look at the seigneur, beckoning him to follow.

If Jean-Pierre was shocked by the wizened housekeeper, he was even more taken aback by his sister-in-law. Even as a girl, she'd turned heads, and as she matured, the headstrong and lusty local gentry made their way to the remote château where she lived. For the most part, she refused to give them an audience and held the king himself at bay when he came sniffing, like many of his lesser subjects. It was said that even the moon and stars favored her, and that at night the castle glowed with an uncommon radiance.

How different was the woman who now waited in a chair in her sitting room, a blanket draped over her lap. The fire that roared in the massive stone hearth threw a heat that seemed to die as it entered the room, its flames flickering against the woman's deeply lined face. Esclarmonde's hair, which had once been black as night, now glistened whitely. Her broad cheekbones stood out, the skin draping to a thin-lipped mouth that was surrounded by grooves, as if she had bitten into something bitter and clung to it stubbornly, in spite of the bad taste.

"Hello, brother," she said, holding out her hand.

Jean-Pierre bent to kiss it lightly. The flesh was soft and cool. Esclarmonde motioned to the housekeeper, Marie, who quietly left the room, but not before stabbing a glance at Jean-Pierre, making it plain she had her eye on him.

Esclarmonde smiled faintly. She gestured toward a nearby chair.

"What brings you to my humble abode?" she asked.

"You sent for me!" he blurted.

Even with a fire in the hearth and a lamp on the table beside Esclarmonde's chair, the room had a darkness that knitted in the corners and seemed to creep out from under the ancient furniture.

"Ah, yes," she murmured.

Jean-Pierre knew that social etiquette required a more subtle approach to the question that burned in him, but he could not contain himself. "Where is my wife?" he demanded.

Esclarmonde recoiled. Her eyebrows climbed her forehead.

"Eleanor? You thought she was here?"

"Isn't that why you wanted to see me?"

Esclarmonde studied him for a long, painful moment.

"You've been gone a long time," she said, cautiously. Her eyes glittered in the firelight. "After you disappeared, and when we heard of the Dragonnades, of course we did what we could. I offered Eleanor and Pierre sanctuary here, with me, where they would have been safe. But my dear sister had a fatal flaw. She believed that a just God would not abandon her. More to the point, she believed in *you*. She never doubted you would return and set things right."

Jean-Pierre bridled.

"What are you saying? Is she here or not?"

"What I'm trying to tell you is that she refused to leave the manoir. Not when she received word that the dragoons were on their way, and not when they arrived and treated the manoir as if it were theirs. Do you know what happens to women on their own, when they fall into the hands of men like that? Do you have any idea what she went through?"

Jean-Pierre was aghast. He shook his head back and forth.

"They wouldn't dare touch a seigneur's wife!"

"Some say an inquisitor wouldn't dare kidnap a nobleman!" she snapped, obviously weary of Jean-Pierre's struggle to accept a truth that she had reconciled herself to a long time ago. Then her fierce mien softened.

"I'm sorry, brother," she finally said.

"Sorry?"

"I can only imagine the circumstances that drove her to the *endura*," she added, referring to the Cathar ritual of willful starvation. "There are some who think it is a good thing, because of the True God who awaits us, and I might have thought the same thing once, when I had a head full of clouds. You remember those days, don't you, when we thought we would live forever and there was so very much that we didn't know?"

Jean-Pierre's head reeled.

"She took the endura?" he gasped.

Esclarmonde had closed her eyes, as if retreating to a secret place where no one could find her. A place she might have shared with her sister, at one time, when two young innocents had hoped and planned and dreamed together.

"She's dead?" Jean-Pierre whimpered.

Esclarmonde raised a hand, which hovered in the gloom like a pale lily. At first, Jean-Pierre thought that she beckoned to him, and tensed to rise from his chair. But then the hand seemed to wilt, and a woman he had not yet seen appeared at his side. She wore her graying hair down, as if prepared for bed. Her face had a papery glow. Jean-Pierre felt a soft touch on his shoulder.

"If it is any comfort, Eleanor sleeps among her roses, where she is safe at last. As for me?" Esclarmonde sighed. "I must rest. I'm afraid our conversation has worn me out. Grace will show you to your room."

"Wait!" Jean-Pierre cried.

Having just learned that his wife was dead and that he may very well have trodden atop her grave, his wits took flight. It took him a few seconds to find the question that he was afraid to ask.

"What of my son? What of Pierre? Is he dead too?"

But by then, Esclarmonde's head had inclined forward until her chin rested on her chest. Jean-Pierre felt Grace's fingers tighten on his shoulder and he rose woodenly to his feet. Out in the much cooler hallway, his knees buckled and he had to catch himself against the nearby wall. A few minutes later, in the cold, empty bed that Esclarmonde had allotted him, he wept. The heavy drapes at the window flickered with a faint light. Thunder boomed, and the hot tears came.

Then, he must have dozed, for the ghosts began to appear. During his incarceration, they had kept him company, filling his dreams at times with terror, but also with a fearsome comfort, for he would rather be haunted than not visited at all. Now, the ghosts stood silent and near, vanishing in the flickering storm light and then reappearing. The men from his guard, murdered so many years ago, gazed at him somberly. His father and mother, his brother, Raymond, who had perished in the Languedoc, while defending a village from marauding northerners, long before the Dragonnades, when religious unrest still flared like an underground fire that broke to the surface now and then. His wife, Eleanor, stood by the bedside looking down on him with pity, one of her hands on the shoulder of a boy who must surely be a man by now, and it was more than Jean-Pierre could bear. The look in the boy's eyes. The blame for Jean-Pierre's failure as a husband and a father. The accusation that knifed him and tore him asunder.

◆　◆　◆

HE AWOKE TO GRAY LIGHT, the taste of ashes in his mouth, and his belly in a knot. He pushed the blanket aside and sat on the edge of the bed, not knowing what to do with himself now. Casting a dull look at a nearby chair, he saw a shirt and trousers, a waistcoat and jacket, all neatly folded. He recognized them as his own, but felt detached, as if they were the borrowed and ill-fitting garments of someone he did not know. He might have sat there until he turned to stone, unable to move or stir, incapable of straightening his knees and rising.

A knock sounded at the door, and Marie poked her head into the room. Those sharp eyes of hers snapped up the situation and her face softened. She marched to the window and opened the drapes, then helped Jean-Pierre dress, buttoning his shirt for him and buckling his trousers. She held the vest while he inserted his arms. It was she who decided that the jacket was not necessary, and she shook out the folds and hung it in the wardrobe along the wall.

"How long have you known?" Jean-Pierre asked, unable to be more specific. For the thought simply wouldn't complete itself.

But Marie understood. She gave one of those sighs that seemed to allow that too much knowledge was sometimes too great a burden. Jean-Pierre had seen the same look on Esclarmonde's face the night before.

"Not much goes on in this land without Madame Esclarmonde's knowledge," she said, busying herself with straightening out the sheets and making the bed. "It is a blessing to be so informed, but it comes at a price. Many's the time Madame has commented that the True God, in his omnipotence, must be the unhappiest of us all."

"And Pierre?" Jean-Pierre implored.

"You must ask Madame," Marie said, gently. "Now come, we must leave this dingy room to the shadows it is used to. We don't get many guests, as you can imagine. Madame is not an easy woman. She took the death of her sister very hard, as you do, I can only imagine. It will do you both good to spend time together."

She took Jean-Pierre's arm and tugged gently. The strength that radiated from her wiry frame amazed him. As a young man, he had always been afraid of her, imagining that she had the evil eye, and now he wondered why. For even though he towered over her, it was she who enabled him to put one foot in front of the other.

Once out of the room, they followed a faded carpet down the length of the hallway. The walls were lined with portraits of personages in the awkward poses of stuffed animals. Eleanor would have known who they were, but they meant nothing to Jean-Pierre. Going down the stairs, he gripped a wooden railing that had been worn smooth by centuries of unknown hands.

In the kitchen, a young woman stood in front of a heavy table that had been gullied from many years of chopping. Holding a knife in one hand and a turnip in the other, she paused in her task and glanced up sharply, giving him the slow, solid probe of a cat that was not entirely certain of its place in an environment subtly altered by a newcomer's presence. But Marie tugged him toward a door that opened onto a courtyard.

A small patch of roses stood in the center of the courtyard, surrounded by cobbles that glittered wetly in the aftermath of last night's storm. Esclarmonde stood among the thorny bushes, inspecting a late-season bloom. She wore a simple black smock and an apron with pockets. As he approached, she raised the flower to her nose and inhaled the fragrance.

"I never liked roses, you know," she said, as if they had already exchanged the usual pleasantries. "Some people think they symbolize love and purity, but I am of a different mind. It's the color red, you see, the color of blood. My family has seen so much of it over the years."

She gestured toward a nearby table. Marie let him go, and he turned to thank her, feeling strangely beholden in a way he could not have described. But she was already shuffling away.

He glanced at the chairs to see if they were dry enough for Esclarmonde to sit on. Bending down, he used his shirtsleeve to wipe away the dew.

"I doubt you slept any better than I did, with the news of Eleanor's passing," Esclarmonde ventured, with the twitch of a grateful nod as she sat. "I assumed you already knew but have to remind myself what a rare commodity knowledge is, how hard it is to come by, and how precious it is to have. Eleanor and I quarreled, you know. She was supposed to take the consolamentum with me, but then you came along and changed everything. I'm afraid the last words I had with her were not very kind."

"She loved you," Jean-Pierre said.

"Did she?" Esclarmonde said, her eyes narrowing as she pushed the thought around in her mind. "Yes, I suppose she did. The way I loved her. But we quarreled nevertheless."

She paused, avoiding his eyes. The maid from the kitchen appeared with a tray that held a pot of herbal tea and pastries. Esclarmonde gave her an appreciative glance, then focused on Jean-Pierre with a look of fierce determination.

"I will tell you everything I know, of course. But first, I have a question for *you*, one that I have struggled with for a long time." She cocked her head, regarding him with the same detached curiosity with which she might have interrogated a stable hand. "I think you might understand more than anyone and may even forgive me for asking, but do you still believe in God, dear brother, after all you've been through? Do you believe he knows who you are and has the slightest concern for your welfare?"

Jean-Pierre tried to weigh the embittered woman in front of him with the ardent youth who had once preferred the True God to the company of men, and who'd taken her vows at such an early age. The consolamentum was not to be taken lightly. It fixed one's eyes on the Holy Spirit and embodied a departure from earthly pleasures. Most Cathars didn't take it until their deathbed.

He hesitated.

"You've changed," he finally observed.

Esclarmonde toyed with her teacup, thoughtfully at first, then with increasing annoyance, as if dark thoughts took over.

"Perhaps I have," she admitted. Her gaze shifted to an armed woman at the edge of the courtyard. "Yes, I think you must be right." She gave a slow, heavy nod. "I am not the person I once was, certainly, when I didn't know better. It is a blessed curse, you know—naïveté. You see through the heart instead of the mind. The heart fills you with hope, but the mind dashes it to pieces. The heart tells you that a life of devotion will bring you closer to God, but the mind reveals a different story. It makes it painfully clear that the world is not in balance and that the strength of one's faith offers protections that only go so far.

"Do you know what attracted me to the Way, back in the very beginning, when I was too young to know better? There were so few of us left. There were still a few *perfecti*, scattered here and there, mostly in hiding. There were a few men, but mostly women, and I thought they were so brave. I thought they were the courageous holdouts of one of the few religions that took women seriously, and that was what I wanted. I wanted to be like them."

She closed her eyes. "But what good was it, in the end?" she breathed. "What good was it to live in the light and follow a path of reason, when those around us entered discourse with their swords and took what they wanted? I should have learned from the Albigensians," she said, referring to the victims of the Cathar Crusade, which happened in the thirteenth century but still lingered in the minds of the few remaining Cathars.

She lifted her hand in a tired wave.

"You of all people should know what it's like to suffer at the hands of another who happens to have the power to harm you. When one person is stronger than another, peace and goodwill require restraint, which is an uncommon thing in the world we live in. A stronger person will use his strength without considering the consequences. You were a nobleman and a courtier, and the inquisitor still abused you. Why? Because he *could*. Think of that. And then think of what it must be like to be one of *them*." Her eyes drifted to the female guard. "Think of what it is like to be *alone* in the world, when the dark clouds gather and the ground shakes and the God you worshipped has turned his back on you."

"They seem pretty formidable to me," Jean-Pierre observed, following her gaze.

"They are well trained, yes, and have strength in their numbers. But it wasn't always this way, and it won't always be enough. There will come a day . . ."

Her tirade seemed to have exhausted her, and she appeared to shrivel. Her face paled and took on a waxy sheen. Her shoulders slumped. She listed sideways in the chair, and Jean-Pierre jumped up and hastened to her side.

A quick glance told him that the female soldier stationed at the edge of the courtyard was already headed in their direction. Another glance informed him that Marie was rushing toward them as well. In the several minutes that followed, he watched the two women tend to their mistress, helping her to her feet and guiding her to the château, which swallowed them up and left the courtyard empty but for him, the stricken seigneur.

Over the next several hours, he anxiously awaited news of her condition. For the most part, he waited in the sitting room, gazing at the paintings of strangers who gazed back through the dark veneer of time. Some of the furniture looked so old that he feared it might collapse if he sat upon it. The only apparent attempt at freshening the room was a vase of roses. But they had wilted and stiffened into floral skeletons. When he couldn't take the gloom any longer, he went outside for some air, and that was where Marie found him, alone in the stables, among the smells of hay and horses. She told him that Esclarmonde was doing much better and hoped to continue their conversation in the library.

Greatly relieved, he followed the housekeeper back inside. First the rose garden and now the library—was it a coincidence that Esclarmonde seemed drawn to places that had been so meaningful to her sister? Jean-Pierre remembered how his wife would sometimes sit with a book on her lap and one of her hands spread across it as if soaking up its contents through her palm. He loved the raptness with which she read, and he could still hear her sighs as she finished a book that she didn't want to put down. Not being a reader himself, he had once asked her why she hid herself between vellum covers and inked pages, and she gave him one of those endearing smiles reserved for people who were still loved in spite of their failings.

"I must apologize," Esclarmonde said, upon his approach, with a chastened mien that sat awkwardly upon such proud shoulders. She patted the seat of a chair next to her. "You have come all this way to get news of your family and I have been less than forthcoming."

"You knew the fate of my wife," he reminded her.

"Yes, of course, but that was not why I asked you here in the first place. You might have noticed that my health is declining," she said, sighing. "When we're young, we talk about our mortality as if it were something destined for someone else. We don't actually think our time will really come." She paused to gaze around the room they sat in, the shelves lined with books and the windows that let in a pale afternoon light. A thin film of grime lay upon the glass, partly obscuring the view outside.

"I would like to make amends," she continued, with a small burst of vigor. "When you took my sister away from me, I was . . . well, I didn't thank you kindly for it, let's just put it that way. My sister and I had a special connection. I don't expect you or anyone else to understand. But I was wrong to be at odds with you, and I don't want to carry it with me to the grave. Marrying you was Eleanor's decision, and I was wrong to blame you.

"More importantly, I would like to pass on some information that will be of vital interest to you. Eleanor may be gone, to our mutual sorrow, but not all is lost. Not for you, anyway. Let me assure you that you are welcome to stay here with me and spend the rest of your days enjoying whatever hospitality I can provide. But you have another option, dear brother, for your son, Pierre, still lives. He's alive, against all odds and the obstacles the Evil One has thrown in his path."

Jean-Pierre listened in stunned silence as she went on to talk of a place called Penn's Woods, where lived a farmer who went by the name of Laux. Esclarmonde said she had dispatched fellow *Bons Chrétiens*—which was one of the names Cathars called themselves— to seek this man out and keep an eye on him. That was how she found out that Jean-Pierre's son had children of his own, including a daughter who was the very image of Eleanor, her grandmother.

The breath left Jean-Pierre's body. He had heard of Penn's Woods and had a vague sense of where it was. But he couldn't imagine a child of his in such a place. America, as some already called it, had little more substance than a nightmare in his mind. It was a place where a certain kind of person went—fur trappers and questionable characters. The kind of person who felt at home in the smoky squalor of a campsite.

"You must go there and find him," Esclarmonde urged.

"How?" he asked, squeezing his eyes shut as the tears bubbled, feeling too old to set out on yet another journey and too weak to make an ocean crossing that had claimed many a far stouter soul.

"How did you get this far?"

Jean-Pierre gawked at her, wondering how much she really knew. Somehow, she had found out about his imprisonment and the foul treatment he had endured, long after the fact, perhaps, but nevertheless. She knew of the inquisitor and how Jean-Pierre's family had fared at the hands of the dragoons that billeted in the manoir. Did this amazing woman, who had spies everywhere, know of the child, too, without whose help he would not have gotten very far at all?

"You look stricken!" Esclarmonde exclaimed.

"I fear I have made a terrible oversight," he said, sick at both heart and soul.

Her look bade him to go on.

"It is too late to make amends," he groaned.

Esclarmonde's eyes sharpened. "How so?" she pressed.

Jean-Pierre gazed at her mournfully.

"He's gone. He was staying in the barracks at the manoir and now he's gone."

Esclarmonde frowned. "Who are you talking about?"

"The boy, Gabriel."

"The boy?"

Her frown deepened and then smoothed.

"You thought that the child you traveled with was a boy?"

Jean-Pierre gave his sister-in-law a blank look that persisted until a quickening thought stunned him. Esclarmonde barked with laughter as she proceeded to tell him what she had learned from the reports that she had received. At first, he couldn't believe what she was saying, but then, when he thought about it, he didn't understand how he couldn't have known all along. What he had to do became clear, along with the sad realization that, no matter what else happened, he would never see Esclarmonde again. Rising from his chair, he bent to kiss her on the cheek, then turned and stumbled from the room.

◆　◆　◆

AT A TIME WHEN TWO continents had the appearance of being joined at the hip, two threads of the same family still knew very little of each other's existence. Jean-Pierre knew virtually nothing about the man once destined to be an old-world seigneur, who now owned a farm on the Pennsylvania frontier. He had never met this man's family and had no way of knowing, for instance, that at this very moment, an officer of the Royal Navy stood in a fog-shrouded field near a place called New York, where the cold morning dew soaked his breeches to the knees. The officer would have been strikingly handsome but for the scar that ran from his left brow across the bridge of his nose and down the opposite cheek.

"Are you sure you want to do this?" said the fellow officer at his side, and Jean Laux didn't respond at first. He had his father's reserve, the tendency to look for light in a surrounding darkness and search for reason if it could be found. But there was, by now, a hardness in him that made him unyielding. He turned a cold, determined eye on his second.

"Proceed," he said, and the other man nodded.

In such moments, little things become very big, like the breath that fluttered around their lips in the cold air, the damp fog that bathed their faces and seemed to crawl down their collars and along their skin. The uncanny quietude of the sodden meadow. The heart that pounded with a rhythm that went all the way back to Jean's youth, when he had taken a position on a mountain ridge and awaited the approach of the outlaws who had kidnapped a local farmgirl. Pennsylvania was still a wild place, and one found unspeakable things where so much darkness prevailed. Perhaps the outlaws intended to sell the girl to the same slave market where they sold captured natives. Perhaps they had other plans for her. All Jean knew at the time was that he alone stood between them and their escape into a backcountry that would give them free rein to exercise whatever they had in mind. This had been the first time Jean ever pointed his weapon at another human being.

Now, across the field from him stood the other man, who also had an attendant, or second. Both of these men wore the same naval uniform as Jean, which made him despise them all the more. Men who abused women were, to Jean, cowards of the worst sort. It didn't matter who the women were—whether they were society women from Boston or the native wives of provincial soldiers.

"She's a savage," the coward had sneered, when Jean first learned of his crime and accosted him with it. "She's no better than a feral hog and her husband's a disgrace." He turned to the side and spat.

"You were the officer in charge," Jean responded, and the man should have taken note of his steely tone.

"He was a colonial, for the love of Jesus," the man barked, and he should have observed the cold, flinty look that entered Jean's eyes.

"I'm a colonial as well," Jean said, quietly, and the man should have paid better attention. His eyes widened, but he otherwise remained rooted, defiant, perhaps thinking Jean's challenge had been spurious and would go no further. "Maybe the woman couldn't defend herself and her husband felt he had no recourse," Jean hissed. "But I am not bound by rank or station, and certainly not by any affection for the likes of you."

The fog tugged and pulled at them now, drifting between the opponents and making them appear as ghosts. Jean could have argued that another man's business was none of his own, if it did not impact him directly. But what the man had done *did* affect him. Jean had saved the kidnapped farmgirl, but then, when it came to his own sister—his own flesh and blood—he had failed. He saw Catharine with her baby in her arms and it still tore a gasp from him, these many years later, long after the assault that had put a tragic end to the lives of both mother and child.

The referee had already offered the choice of pistols to the other man and now approached Jean with the wooden box. Jean waved for his second to take the remaining pistol, which he did. The second inserted a short rod into the barrel to make sure a ball was not already seated. Then he deftly loaded the weapon and held it out to Jean.

The pistol was cold and hard in his hand, a heft of several pounds. Fog beaded on the barrel, making it glisten. The opponents faced each other. At a command from the referee, they raised their weapons. But something went wrong. Before the referee gave the command to fire, Jean's opponent pulled his trigger, and his gun erupted in a deafening thunderclap. A cloud of burnt powder issued across the field and a sudden pain burst from the side of Jean's head where his ear had been. Then, in a flurry of motion, Jean's opponent tossed his pistol aside and grasped at another that his associate hurriedly offered him. He hauled back on the hammer, frantic with haste, then raised the weapon for another shot.

Jean stood with his own pistol extended. He had not flinched when the other man's bullet took off part of his ear, and he paid no attention to the hot blood that now ran down his neck and soaked the collar of his uniform. He often thought of his sister in her final moments, facing a man three times her size, and a violent rage consumed him. The shakes would come later, as they always did, but for now, his aim was rock steady. He only wished Catharine could be behind him—she and her little bitty baby, the both of them safe and sound—as he pulled the trigger.

THIRTEEN

The sun was already heating up when Gotzone heard the tough, boyish voice. She had slept next to the rock she had sat on the previous night, and dry grass clung to her hair. Dirt stuck to the side of her face. The boy stood over her, looking down, with two other boys behind him.

"Look what we have here," he said, derisively, and it took a moment for Gotzone to wake up enough to understand what was happening. That nighttime had turned to day and that the stiff, deeply chilled conjunction of aching bones was the body she had awakened to.

The boy smirked at his mates.

"Who is she?" one of the other boys said.

Like the first one, he wore rags and his eyes had a cold, suspicious look.

"Does it matter?" the third boy responded, leering.

"I'm not afraid of you," Gotzone said, struggling to her feet. She wore only a shift and had bare feet, but balled her fists nevertheless. With a small tug of wonder, she realized she was not afraid, and that she would never be again, for fear was another way of dying and she was determined to give up her ghost but once. She knew she didn't stand a chance against the three of them. But they would have to take from her whatever it was they wanted, and take the devil in the process.

The boys studied her in their cruel, probing manner, perhaps unsettled by her defiance and momentarily unsure of themselves. One of them sniggered. Then, the most amazing thing happened. They looked up and their faces went blank. The craftiness and meanness fled. One stepped backward and another followed suit. Then the third did the same, tripped, and almost fell, and Gotzone had the awareness that something had changed, like the shadow of a cloud crossing the sun. She turned and her jaw dropped.

"How are you boys doing—seeking a little merriment, are we?" François Aguirre said, sarcastically. He sat astride a towering horse, wearing a sword at his side and a pistol in his belt. Nudging his horse, he guided it past Gotzone and toward the boys, his face set with grim pleasure. She had no doubt that François would have trampled the boys if they didn't scramble out of the way.

"Merde!" one cried.

"*Sacre!* . . ." cursed another.

François goaded the horse and the boys fled, scattering in different directions. He let out a frightening bark of laughter. Then he sobered, turning the horse around to face Gotzone.

"*You!*" she cried, the word flying from her mouth, remembering him from the manoir.

"Have we met?" he asked, feigning ignorance, appearing to enjoy her confusion as much as he had the fright he had given the boys. Without waiting for a response, he swung down off his mount, then untied one of his saddlebags and took out something wrapped in cloth. Squatting down, he opened the package and placed a piece of cheese on the rock that Gotzone had slept beside. He took a knife from his pocket and sliced a wedge.

"What're you doing here?" Gotzone gasped.

François looked down at the cheese in his hand, as if loath to respond. And in fact, he didn't have to answer, for it soon became obvious that he would only have acted at the behest of one other. Gotzone watched him pop the morsel into his mouth.

"Did Jean-Pierre send you? Did he know? . . ."

François chewed solemnly, then cocked his head to the side, as if carried aloft by a sudden thought.

"Know what? That you were not what you appeared to be?"

He shrugged, and Gotzone blanched. To hear her deception put so bluntly into words made her stomach twist into a knot.

François's eyes narrowed, as if in thought. "Do you believe in *hasard*?" he asked.

"I don't know what you're talking about," Gotzone groused.

"It's a word the French use, meaning luck," François said, nodding in the general direction of the north. "It's one of their more positive contributions, though I will deny I ever said it if anyone asks. It's their word for luck, like I said—but it means more than that. Some say it is the way God offers us choices in order to help us out and maybe get a little bit of what he wants in the process.

"But in answer to your question, how should I know what the seigneur knew? Seigneurs are . . . well, they're who they are, for better or worse, and maybe you just got lucky. But he seems to have plans for you. He said that he already lost one child and that he isn't going to lose another."

He sliced a second piece of cheese and this time held it out to her. Getting up, he went to his saddlebag and returned with a bladder of wine. He tipped his head back, letting the wine stream into his mouth, and some of it dribbled down his chin. After she took a turn with the bladder, he wrapped up what was left of the cheese and then returned it and the wine to the saddlebag. He placed his boot in the nearby stirrup and swung up into the saddle.

Reaching down, he held out a hand.

Gotzone bridled. "What makes you think I'd go anywhere with you?"

He grinned, which annoyed her to no end. She stewed on her options, muttering some of the words she had heard while in the company of men.

"The least you can do is look away," she said.

Grunting as if it meant nothing to him, he did as she asked. She eyed him suspiciously but then relented, bunching the hem of her dress and then taking his hand. He removed his foot from the stirrup so that she could use it to swing up behind him. It took some effort, but she was finally situated.

François grinned. "I didn't get to spend much time with Gabriel, but I'd wager he wasn't half the fuss that you are."

"Just mind your business," she retorted.

Her body unavoidably pressed against his, and at first, the contact revolted her. A flutter of panic ripped through her. But François seemed oblivious, guiding the horse along the road with an easy grace, and Gotzone began to relax. Each step of the horse thrust her body against the powerful figure she clung to and gradually her discomfort subsided. Before long she dozed, dreaming she was a cloud in the sky, with nothing to do but drift along.

◆　◆　◆

As François guided the horse around the final bend and down the hill into San Sebastian, Gotzone gasped. She had never seen the ocean before, and the startling blue of the Bay of Biscay poked her in the eye. The sunlight that danced off the water made her dizzy. Everything seemed new and fresh. Jean-Pierre stood in front of a whitewashed villa. The transformation he had undergone at the manoir had been more than enough to convince her that she no longer belonged in his life, and now, the man she had once presumed to be a vagabond wore a white shirt with ballooning sleeves, a brocaded waistcoat, fawn trousers, and blue leather slippers. As the travelers neared, he held out his hands as if welcoming dear and long-lost souls that he had almost given up the hope of ever seeing again.

Clinging to François throughout the journey, Gotzone had rehearsed this moment over and over again—what she would say to this man she had once thought she knew. It was not like meeting him for the first time, when she might form a fresh impression. Indeed, she had no faith that the seigneur was not somehow leading her astray, somehow misleading her and fooling her now as another had once done. Jean-Pierre gave her a quick tour of the villa, pointing out one of the rooms that he called hers, then whisked her off to a bathhouse, where female patrons were normally forbidden. Jean-Pierre soon had the building cleared, and Gotzone found herself in the luxury of a tub of hot water.

The only other time in her life she had had a hot bath was when she lived with the priest. Back then, the bath was a prelude to something else that she didn't want to think about, and as much as she enjoyed the steaming water, she found it hard to suppress the hammering of her heart. Female attendants hovered near, and Gotzone crossed her arms against her chest, embarrassed to be naked in front of strangers. But the women took no notice of her discomfort. They washed her hair and scrubbed her back with a long-handled brush, taking her gently by the wrist and moving her arms this way and that. One of the women brought a thick cotton robe and cloth sandals that absorbed Gotzone's body warmth and enveloped her in a cocoon of comfort.

Back in the dressing area, she found her old dress had been taken away and a new one lay in its place. The breath left her body, for the new dress was of silk. It came with a jacket of teased fabric that looked like white fur, and there were white leather sandals. Her amazement turned to fear as the women insisted on dressing her. One of them brushed out her hair, which by now reached to her shoulders, and her fear turned like a piece of broken glass in her chest, for in the past, such attention had only meant one thing.

Then, when Jean-Pierre took her to dinner, she was sure that all was lost. They sat on a terrace overlooking the sparkling blue of the bay, while a man in livery brought dishes of roasted meats with butter sauces, a fish with cracking skin, and then lamb that looked like small circles of rosy flesh on long, blackened rib bones, that had been marinated in herbs and mustard. Having never had such a succulent meal, she could only imagine the very personal price to be paid.

"Why am I here?" she finally found the courage to ask. Truly, it didn't seem to matter anymore that she had masqueraded as someone she was not and fooled the seigneur for so long. Already that part of her life seemed far behind her.

Jean-Pierre waved his hand and their server departed. He soberly studied the young woman who sat across from him, and his eyes seemed to grow in intensity.

"We are not so different, the two of us," he said.

Gotzone shook her head vigorously.

"How can you say that?" she asked.

"Hear me out, please," he urged. His gaze drifted to look around the terrace, the tables with white coverings, the fine China and silver service, the white balustrade, the expansive airiness of the sea and sky that lay beyond. Leaning forward in his chair and speaking in a hoarse whisper, he related what his sister-in-law, Esclarmonde, had told him about his son, Pierre, who now lived in the New World, across that very sea. Grimacing, he spoke of the colonies as if they were a curse, rather than lands of opportunity.

"So there you have it," Gotzone said, with a bitterness that she couldn't hold back. "You have found the family that you sought, and I am happy for you. That's all you cared about, anyway. So go to them!"

Fighting a flood of tears, she placed her hands on the table and started to rise. But Jean-Pierre placed his big hand on one of hers, restraining her.

"You don't understand," he said.

"What's to understand?"

"*Chere*, I can't do it alone," he lamented. "You have had to grow up too fast and I'm sorry, but there is an answer to the dilemma that both of us face. There is nothing left here for either one of us, but we are not without direction or resources. Now that we're together again, we can help each other."

Gotzone stiffened.

"If you're saying what I think you are, then the answer's no. I will not share another man's bed, not yours or anyone else's—never again!" she exclaimed, tugging her hand free from his.

Jean-Pierre's eyes widened. He looked stricken.

"Why would you say such a thing?" he said.

"Because. Just because, that's why!"

"But—"

"Because I know what men want!" she sobbed.

Jean-Pierre reared back in his chair.

"But you don't understand!" he protested. "What I propose to do is to make you my daughter!"

Gotzone searched the seigneur's face, where the truth of his words pressed against the seawall of hazel eyes. She didn't know what his words meant, how he could endeavor to make her his daughter when she had not been born to him in the first place. She had never heard of such a thing. Looking at him, she saw still the frightening strength of a man, but something else as well. Something she might have found easier to trust, in a different time and place, if she weren't the person she had become.

He didn't press her for an answer just then. He said to think about it, and later, back in her room at the villa, she lay awake long into the night, replaying the conversation over and over in her mind, trying to understand what Jean-Pierre was offering her and looking for any signs whatsoever that she was being deceived. The window was open to the night air and the curtains stirred like diaphanous skirts. Moonlight spilled across the floor. The pillow smelled faintly of lavender, and as the cool breeze crept over her like an unbidden lover, she had the wild sensation of being alone at sea, adrift in the dark and at the mercy of unknown currents.

◆　◆　◆

YEARS LATER, GOTZONE WOULD SAY she had little choice but to accept Jean-Pierre's offer. He was already a better friend than she had ever had, and hasard had brought them together when neither one had the wherewithal to stand on their own. True, the seigneur could have retreated to his manoir, continued to harvest his lost belongings from the people of his village, and eked out a life of sorts. But with his wife gone and his son living in a foreign land, his inner vitality would have shriveled, and the wounds inflicted by the cardinal those many years ago would have turned fatal at last.

That said, Gotzone's new life launched with hardly a pause. Jean-Pierre informed her that they would have to wait for suitable passage to the place he called America, which could be difficult, he allowed, as San Sebastian was considered Spanish territory, at the time, while the American Colonies were English, and the twain were at odds. But she hardly had a chance to settle in at the villa before a horse drew a wagon to the door. A young woman sat on the bench next to the portly driver. She wore a bonnet and a heavy shawl over a cotton dress and sat holding a cloth bag in her lap. Gotzone watched from the door of the villa as Jean-Pierre helped the woman down.

"Gotzone, I would like you to meet Molly Banks, your tutor," Jean-Pierre said, beaming.

"My what?"

"You're my daughter now, and I will not have you be ignorant," he replied, sternly, watching the wagoner drag a heavy trunk past him into the house. The man had unbuttoned his coat, for he perspired heavily despite the chill grip of late autumn.

Jean-Pierre led Gotzone aside and lowered his voice.

"Where we are going, they don't speak the tongues you are used to," he said. "They speak what is called the English, and Molly will show you how to read and write the way they do it in America. She will even teach you ciphering, for . . ." He paused to make sure he had her full attention. "I will not be around forever, and you must be prepared to carry on without me. You must know how to express yourself and you must know when you are being cheated, so that you can protect yourself."

Gotzone nodded as if she understood. But of course, she didn't know what he was saying, for how could she? Very few people could read and write, and she failed to understand what set her apart and why the education that Jean-Pierre spoke of mattered.

The first book Molly used as a lexicon was the Bible, which frightened Gotzone to death, for she couldn't imagine the voice of God being trapped in the little cages that Molly called words. They sat by a window in the villa, where a pale light spilled through.

"Behold, I send my messenger before thy face," Molly read aloud, turning ink marks into sounds.

Gotzone's eyes widened with wonder.

"They're just words," Molly laughed.

Gotzone leaned forward.

"But aren't they the words of . . ."

Glancing around to make sure even Jean-Pierre couldn't hear, Gotzone stabbed a forefinger upward, and Molly shook her head with barely suppressed mirth. She waved a hand dismissively.

"Let's just go ahead and start with 'behold,'" she went on. "It is a word in English meaning to gaze upon or look at. Then, there is the word 'messenger,' which means a person who carries out the behest of another, such as when the seigneur tells you what to say to some- one else." She then went on to explain the properties of the words in between, the nominative nature of one, the action of the second, and the possessive of another.

"You mean 'I' and 'my' mean the same thing?" Gotzone said, bewildered.

"Almost," Molly agreed, with a burst of breath that made Gotzone feel as if she had accomplished something. "We are making headway!"

"But how will I ever learn to read like you?" Gotzone cried, weighing the eight words she had just experienced against the veritable tome that lay open on her tutor's lap, thinking there must be more words in the book than cobbles on the road outside.

"I'm afraid we will have time aplenty," Molly sighed. She reached out a hand to grasp one of Gotzone's. "Who knows when the seigneur will secure passage on a ship? It could take months or even years. Between the two of us, I doubt a passage to Philadelphia will even be found. You will have to go to someplace like La Florida and then figure out what to do next in order to get to your destination. In the meantime, we have much to do and much to accomplish, and you are already doing well!"

Gotzone studied her tutor in an attempt to divine meaning from her eyes or expressions—anything to assist in her understanding of what Molly was saying. The way Molly articulated the challenges that lay ahead made them sound formidable indeed. And then there were the concerns that Gotzone already had, and which bothered her like biting ants. She felt many things for Jean-Pierre, but faith in his well-being was not one of them. She remembered the doddering vieux she had met on the road from Toulouse and the man she subsequently found collapsed in the manoir, when Jean-Pierre forced an entry, only to discover the emptiness that lay inside. She feared that the man she now called her father was in failing health. What would she do if he didn't make it to the Penn's Woods that had become such an irrevocable object of their hopes and dreams? What would become of them if they got to Philadelphia and couldn't locate this Pierre? What would become of Jean-Pierre, and no less importantly, what would become of her?

"Show me more words," she said to Molly, her head throbbing, for her concerns did not get her very far, one way or another. Whether or not she would have died if Jean-Pierre had not sent François to rescue her didn't seem to matter. She had given up that life. Hasard had given her a new one, and whatever vitality she had left was inextricably tied with that of the seigneur.

"Teach me more of this new language, this English," she said, avoiding her tutor's thoughtful gaze.

FOURTEEN

Magdalena hauled the linens off her bed and piled them in the hallway outside the door. Then she went to her husband's room. He hadn't been home in over a fortnight, occupied as he was with his legislative duties in Philadelphia, but Magdalena was in a frenzy of housecleaning and she added his linens to her pile. The letter from the governor of Antigua indicated that the arrival of the seigneur and his daughter was imminent, which was vague at best. Due to the travel vagaries of the time, the voyage from Antigua to Philadelphia could take anywhere from four days—which was highly unlikely—to several weeks. Adding to the uncertainty, the governor had not actually specified a departure date, which meant that they could already be en route, for all she knew, and could show up at any time.

The governor had called out Gotzone by name, as if she were more of a force to be reckoned with than the seigneur, and the name hovered in Magdalena's mind like an apparition. *What kind of name is that?* she wondered, carrying the armload of linens to the laundry room, where a tub of steaming water waited. Magdalena was aware that her own surname was Occitan in origin, not French, because it was a point her father, Pierre, had repeatedly made over the years, as if it were an important distinction. Was Gotzone another departure from what most people thought of as French?

Magdalena's thoughts were interrupted by the bellowing of her dog, Remus, outside in the yard. The thunderous sound struck alarm into the bones of a woman who spent most of her time alone, and she hurried to the foyer window, where she half-expected to see the seigneur on her doorstep. Instead, she saw a woman standing with her hands crossed over her chest, while the big mastiff crouched in front of her. Magdalena knew the woman as Isabelle, though over the course of her many visits, she had never come to the château alone. She was usually in the company of one if not two others.

Not now, of all times, Magdalena thought, blowing out a breath to compose herself before unbolting the door and yanking it open.

"Remus, down!" she shouted, and the dog turned to give her one of those questioning looks that only animals can fully accomplish.

"*Paix*," Isabelle said, her rigid expression breaking with relief. She uncrossed her arms but still held them aloft as she edged her way around the dog. Remus followed close on her heel, and the woman nervously watched him.

"I don't think he remembers me," she said, as she entered the house.

"Of course he remembers you," Magdalena chided, fanning her face with a hand and trying to calm down. She could use a rest anyway, she thought, and what would it hurt to spend some time with an old friend?

She showed Isabelle into the sitting room. A hot kettle still sat on the hearth in the kitchen, and she fetched her visitor a cup of tea.

"Oh, thank you," Isabelle said, receiving the mug gratefully. She sat in Magdalena's usual chair and clasped her mug with both hands in her lap.

"Will Margaret and Timothy be along as well?" Magdalena asked, lowering herself into the chair usually reserved for Lawrence, on the few occasions he was home.

Isabelle's face sagged.

"Well, no, sadly," she said. "It's been two years since we had occasion to call, and a lot has happened. Margaret was the first to go. She took a fever and then the True God took her to his bosom. How cruel, when Timothy took ill as well. One day he was fine and then everything changed." A tear beaded in the corner of her eye. "I have been alone these past six months, and I fear the Lord will soon take me, too. It was all I could do to make this one last effort to see you and offer whatever blessings I have left."

Magdalena placed her cup on the nearby end table next to her book and reached out a hand. Isabelle's fingers were warm from the hot tea, but the wrist above them was as cold as water from the springhouse. Magdalena felt a flutter of distress.

"They have returned to their God, then—where they belong," she offered.

But Isabelle showed little sign of comfort.

"I know I should not feel this way, but I got so used to their company," she said, wiping her eye with the back of her hand. She lifted her gaze to sweep the room, with the painting of a French peasant woman stooped over a sheath of wheat grass and another of one of Lawrence's sawmills, the waterwheel that turned the blade and a workhorse standing patiently in wagon traces. The two works of art represented moments that were worlds apart that had come together in this frontier château.

"I should feel happy for them, because all we ever wished for was to be free from the Evil One's grasp. But I feel as if a boot heel is pressing against my heart. I'm sorry to burden you with this. It is yet another sign of weakness on my part!"

"No . . ." Magdalena murmured, trying to soothe her friend. She was taken aback, to be sure, for the Cathars professed to see death as a release and nothing to be sorrowful about. Indeed, stories abounded of the courage of Cathar parfaites during the abominable crusade, when Montségur fell to the northerners and Cathars were offered a choice between conversion and death. It was said that not only did the parfaites and their male counterparts not capitulate, but that they threw themselves joyfully on the bonfires the crusaders had prepared.

"I am sorry to be such a disappointment," Isabelle went on. "I have come to give you a blessing and here I am begging mercies!"

Magdalena left her chair and knelt in front of her old friend. Isabelle moved her mug out of the way, and Magdalena placed her head on the other woman's lap. She felt the light pressure of Isabelle's hands on her head.

Then, she stood up, taking Isabelle's hands and helping her to her feet. Guiding her to the nearby sofa, Magdalena slid down beside the other woman, holding onto her fiercely before relaxing her grip.

"Will you pray with me?" she asked, and Isabelle nodded, her eyes still reddened and her face damp.

"That would please me," she said.

Magdalena eased back on the sofa, her eyes closed and her hands now in her lap, with the palms turned up. She had always loved meditating with the visiting Cathars, as an inner space seemed to open up to her that gave a deeper meaning to her existence. But now, with Margaret and Timothy both gone and with Isabelle struggling with their loss, that inner peace eluded her. Certainly, one was bound to miss dearly beloved friends when they departed on such an irrevocable journey as death. But Isabelle's mourning seemed to go beyond that. She seemed fearful of her own mortality, and this was what Magdalena did not understand. The Cathars professed a belief that their mortal coil stood between them and an ecstatic reunion with their God, and Magdalena did not understand the crisis of faith that Isabelle now seemed to face.

Isabelle stayed at the château for five days, speaking with her protégé and spending much of the rest of the time in prayer. As the days progressed, the two women had less and less to talk about and spent more time in shared silence. Finally, Isabelle said she had to leave. She didn't say she had other places to go, as she had so often in the past. As far as Magdalena knew, there were no other Cathars in the region. Isabelle's hope for a new-world flock had not materialized in the face of an aggressive Protestantism. Perhaps it was the environment. Maybe the shadow of the dark forest on the edge of the frontier favored a more male-driven religious culture. In any case, as Magdalena watched Isabelle depart, a wan foreboding closed on her heart and she was sure she would never see her friend again.

◆　◆　◆

IN THE WAKE OF ISABELLE'S departure, Magdalena didn't know what to do with herself. The château seemed emptier than ever, and she found herself sometimes standing still, be it in the kitchen or the sitting room—even the mudroom, where her outdoor boots sat on a rack against the wall—feeling the stillness around her. The house made sounds that she knew to be the shifting of timbers and beams as the temperature fluctuated outside, as if having once lived, the wood had a hard time letting go of the wild lifeblood that had coursed through it. Perhaps, in its own way, the house was as unsettled as she was, she thought. Any day now, a carriage could pull up in the yard carrying a man whose blood she carried, and what would he find? A woman alone in a house too big for her? Someone lost in the arcane rituals of a dead religion? A married woman who clung to an excuse to remain celibate? What was she afraid of, she asked herself, as she sat in the cavernous great room, rubbing her thumbs against Remus's ears and gazing into his soulful eyes.

She thought she heard something and gasped, but it was nothing, otherwise Remus would have barked. It is said that one of the tragedies of old age is that one feels young in spite of the advancing years, and yet, Magdalena felt the opposite. Barely twenty, she could see the years ahead as if they already lay behind her. Still youthful, she felt withered and old, as if Isabelle were already long gone and she, herself, were soon to follow.

Remus gazed at her as if he knew all her secrets and forgave her, and she gave his thick neck an extra aggressive scratching.

"We must have a holiday," she said.

Remus woofed.

Not wanting to show up at the farm empty-handed, she searched the pantry, where she found a loaf of bread and a jar of wild berry jam she had preserved last year and never got around to eating. She lined a small basket with a cloth napkin and placed the food inside. Then she found her traveling shawl, which hung on a hook in the mudroom. Remus pranced at her heels.

"Of course you'll come with, silly!" Magdalena chided. "Where would I go without you?"

The dog's woof turned into a yip of joy.

Even the horse seemed eager to leave the estate behind, with all of its haunts and grim forebodings. The spirited animal pulled the wagon with a little extra vigor, now and then turning its head to the side as if to make sure it had not gotten things wrong. Remus loped on ahead, his tongue lashing the air, and Magdalena felt like a canine companion that ran at his side.

"Hello?" Beatrice said, holding a paring knife in her hand, as Magdalena burst in through the farmhouse door. A half-dozen carrots lay on the kitchen counter in front of her.

"I just thought I'd pay a visit," Magdalena said, breathlessly, placing her basket of bread and jam on the table.

"Is everything all right?" Beatrice asked, her eyes narrowing.

"Oh, Mother, honestly!" Magdalena said. "Can't I visit the house I was born in? Where's Georgie? Where are the children? I feel like I haven't seen them in ages!"

Beatrice looked at her daughter reprovingly, as if she suspected all was not well. Those deep dark eyes of hers were worse than Remus's when it came to tugging at the truth, and Magdalena had to look away. She yanked open a drawer and pulled out one of her mother's extra aprons.

"Why don't I take care of the carrots while you do something else?"

"You know that you can talk to me," Beatrice said.

"Talk about what?"

"Oh, I don't know, anything. Like what this visit is all about, for instance."

"You do exasperate me sometimes!" Magdalena sighed, shaking her head.

But Beatrice could be every bit as stubborn as Magdalena. She placed the paring knife on the counter next to the carrots and wiped her hands on her apron.

"Why don't we go out on the porch and sit for a while?" she said. "I wouldn't mind getting off my feet for a minute or two." She gave her daughter one of those sideways glances that Magdalena remembered all too well.

On the porch, seven chairs were lined up against the wall of the house, just as they had always been, as far back as Magdalena could remember. Each family member had their own particular spot, and Catharine's chair still stood among the rest, as if in mute defiance of the event that had stolen her life. The two women took their respective seats.

Remus tussled with his littermate out in the yard, growling with mock ferocity. He had the other dog's ear in his mouth, tugging and pulling.

"We've all been a little on edge, what with the seigneur coming," Beatrice suggested. Magdalena had never had the kind of relationship with her mother that she shared with her father, and in one of those rare moments of emotional clarity, she saw her mother for the unique person she was and realized the older woman felt as awkward in this moment as she did.

"I worry about Pa," Magdalena said. "He seems different since we found out about the seigneur. And then there's this girl, this *Gotzone*, who claims to be his sister. As wonderful as it must be to find out that his father is alive, it must be difficult to discover the seigneur had this whole other family."

"Your father's just fine, dear," Beatrice replied. She reached out a hand that had sought chicken eggs from under setting hens, wielded hoes, and pulled weeds, a hand calloused from the use of paring knives against the tough fibers of garden vegetables. When she wasn't working on the farm, shoulder to shoulder with her husband, Beatrice made the meals and cleaned the house. At one point, she'd done the washing for seven people. Even now, with Catharine gone and Jean serving in the Royal Navy and Andrew living off on his own, she still did most of the laundry for Georgie and his family, as well as for herself and Pierre.

"You're the one I worry about," she admitted, clasping Magdalena's hand and giving it a squeeze. "I worry that you're not happy.

How you choose to live your life is your own business and none of mine," she went on. "But it's unnatural to be so alone when you don't have to be."

She sighed.

"As for your father and all this business about the seigneur, it is taking its toll on him, as you well know. Even as a child, you were different, in a special kind of way. You always wanted to take care of other people and make things better for them, but this is something you're going to have to let him deal with on his own. He thought his father was dead and, dare I say it, blamed the man for what happened to his mother. That's old-world business. Would that it had left us alone, but it didn't and it's no use crying about it. Your father's happy that the seigneur's alive. But it's far more complicated than that and you will just have to let him come to terms with it himself."

"But I worry—"

"Of course you do, dear. We all do. But if you really want to help him, you can put your own house in order. It would be a blessing to him, dear one. It would be a blessing to us all."

Magdalena felt the tug of resistance that her mother often seemed to cause, for who likes to have her decisions put under a light, looked at and challenged? But Beatrice gazed out at the yard as if seeing things that only she could perceive, and Magdalena's heart melted. Beatrice's face had many more lines than the image of her that Magdalena held in her mind. Her skin had sagged and softened with age, and Magdalena felt a sharp little pain in her chest.

The two women might have shared their moment a bit longer, and who knows what might have been said and mulled over, and where it might have led? But just then, Georgie Junior strode through the wire gate. At eight, he was filled with the swaggering juice of a little man. He was shirtless, and his upper body was covered with hayseed from the harvest underway. Standing in front of the porch, he glowered at the two women, as if challenging their idleness when so much hard work needed to be done.

Then, shaking his head like a bull calf, he lurched forward and stomped across the porch and into the house.

"Straight to the back, where I have a tub of water waiting for you, young man," Beatrice called after him. "I won't have you tracking dirt around the house or sitting down on anything until after you've had a good bath!"

She tilted her head, listening for a response, and then, when none was forthcoming, relaxed and gave a snort. Magdalena's throat tickled and she let out a similar sound. The two women looked at each other and Beatrice convulsed a little, then started to laugh. Soon, both were howling, rocking in their chairs as they tried to suppress their mirth. Beatrice bunched the hem of her apron and used it to dab at her eyes, and Magdalena pulled a small handkerchief from a pocket in her dress.

Sighing, Beatrice invited Magdalena to stay for supper, and the younger woman was sorely tempted. But as good as the visit had been, there was still something missing. Catharine's empty chair spoke to her, and a short time later, Magdalena pulled the wagon to the side of the road on the crest of a small hill that overlooked the château. This was where she'd first seen the smoking ruins of the original château as a young child, and she clutched her skirt as she picked her way through the brush to the small pile of rocks that memorialized the spot. Woven among the stones were colorful pieces of fabric from Catharine's favorite dress, tufts of hair from Catharine's brush, a baby rattle and a small silver spoon with the name Peter scratched on the handle. Magdalena fell to her knees, clasping her hands together and lowering her forehead to them. People used to tell her that time would heal her wounds. But she didn't think such a thing was possible—not all the time in the world and not these kinds of wounds. A breeze tugged at her hair, and she thought it was so unfair that she was there to feel it and that her sister was not.

Standing up, she brushed the dried grass and dust from her clothing and glanced in the direction of the château, with its turrets and bold architecture, and that was when she saw the rider, approaching along the road from the southeast. Even at a distance, there was something familiar about him, the broad set of shoulders, the casual way he held the reins. He wore an English naval uniform, which wasn't unheard of in this part of the colony, but it was not at all common, either.

When she got to the barn, she saw a black horse with a white blaze on its forehead in one of the stalls, standing there as if it owned the place. Magdalena's hands trembled as she unhitched the wagon and gave her horse a quick rubdown. The edifice that she lived in loomed in front of her, and thrusting open the front door, she felt as if she were trespassing in her own home. Even the air felt different, as if what had once belonged to her had changed its mind about whatever agreement had bound them together and opened its arms to include someone else.

A tall man stood in front of the window in the sitting room, looking out onto Lawrence's vineyard. He wore a scarlet jacket with blue lapels, white breeches, and white stockings. When he turned to look at her, she shuddered at the sight of the scar that angled across his face, and the ear that appeared to be missing.

"Jean!" Magdalena cried.

The officer took a hesitant step toward her, and she rushed into his arms. They embraced and she smelled the pungent fabric of his uniform, then the more familiar smells of his hair and skin, the lingering fragrance of soap, the essence of the boy she had once known.

"Maggy," he breathed, crushing her to him and holding her close, as her aching heart emptied into tears of joy.

FIFTEEN

The following morning, Magdalena awakened to the rich, densely layered aroma of fresh-brewed coffee. It took her a moment to clear the fog from her head. So much of the night before had seemed like a dream, the musings and laughter, the gentle way a brother teased his sister, and the unfolding of joy throughout the evening. She hadn't gone to bed until the early hours, and even then, as tired as she was, she still had difficulty letting go of the unexpected pleasure of an unanticipated reunion.

Slipping into her dressing gown, she went downstairs barefooted and found Jean at one of the kitchen benches, holding a small wire mesh in one hand while he poured a dark, scalding liquid from a kettle with the other. He was fully dressed, with a blousy shirt and the same white breeches he had worn upon his arrival. His suspenders hung down loosely and he stood in stockinged feet. So intent was he on what he was doing that he didn't glance up until the last minute.

"Good morning!" he said, with a grin.

Magdalena blushed, feeling the warmth creep up into her scalp. She had given her hair a quick brushing, but had little confidence that her morning appearance was anything special to behold.

"Did you sleep well?" she inquired.

Jean paused, letting the contents of the kettle slow to a dribble. He cocked his head, as if the question required an unaccustomed amount of concentration.

"I believe I did, yes," he said. "Life in the military has taught me many things, and one of them is a profound appreciation for a warm bed in a safe place." His eyes softened. "Many's the night I've drifted off thinking of you, wondering how you were getting on."

Magdalena nodded. She could only imagine her brother's thoughts, given his complicated relationship with the château. As a young man, he had helped build the original structure. He had worked alongside Lawrence back when he was still married to Catharine, but then, in the aftermath of the tragedy, Jean swore he would never enter the château again and left for England while the reconstruction was still underway.

"And here you are!" Magdalena said.

"Yes," he agreed, but with such soberness that it froze Magdalena's heart. He couldn't seem to look at her and turned his attention to the coffee mugs in front of him.

"You're probably more of a tea drinker," he observed, setting the kettle down on a potholder next to the mortar and pestle he had used to grind the beans. He set the wire mesh down next to the pot. "But I knew Lawrence likes coffee and wanted him to have some," he continued, gesturing toward the bulging cloth sack that sat on the counter. "I'm sure he won't mind if we help ourselves," he added, with a grin.

Then he grew serious and cleared his throat.

"I had something different in mind for you," he said, shooting a glance at her. He fished in the pocket of his shirt and pulled out a shiny object. It was a brooch made of silver, with a blue stone set in the middle.

"Why, Jean, it's lovely!" Magdalena said, holding the brooch as if it were a freshly laid egg she was afraid of breaking.

"I hope you don't mind I didn't wrap it—I'm not very good at that sort of thing." Jean looked abashed. "And I know you're not much of one for adornments."

"Thank you," she said, clasping the brooch and standing on her toes to kiss him on the cheek. The sensation of his whiskers gave her a flutter and she thought she was going to cry.

Jean carried the two mugs to the table, then helped Magdalena with her chair before seating himself.

"You didn't have to bring gifts, you know," Magdalena said. "Your presence is the most precious gift of all!"

Jean gave her a nod that expressed his appreciation, but which at the same time made it clear his mind was made up.

"I thought I would give my horse to Pa. Ma's the tough one. She's so hard on herself and gets in such a huff if you try to make her happy. But I found a nice scarf she might like, something she can wear to church on Sundays. She still goes to that Reformed Church in Watertown, doesn't she?"

Magdalena rolled her eyes in agreement.

"And then there's Andrew and Georgie, along with Georgie's family, of course. I know Andrew is fond of whiskey and that's what I got him—something a little easier on the palate, I dare say, than the stuff that comes out of the hills around here. I got Georgie a knife you can fold and stick in your pocket, and then, I don't know, I kind of ran out of ideas and ended up getting cacao beans for Rachel, that she can use to make a chocolate beverage for her and the children."

"What's going on, Jean?" Magdalena asked, her heart now thumping like a horse's hooves.

"Why, nothing," Jean said, evasively.

"Tell me." She slid her hand forward and placed it on one of his.

Jean sighed. He stared at the table for several seconds. Raising his eyes to meet hers, he quickly glanced away.

"Well, if you must know . . ." he said, then went on to tell her about his duel with a fellow officer and the disturbance the encounter had caused in London. Somehow, Jean had overcome the stigma of being a colonial enough to gain entrance into the Royal Navy—with the help of family connections, he was quick to add. But it did not sit well with some of his superiors that the man he'd killed was a member of the British homeland aristocracy. The man's father was a peer of the realm.

"You killed someone in a duel?" Magdalena gasped. She feared she might throw up.

"He raped the wife of one of his subordinates, another colonial, like me, who had spent time in the American backcountry and married a native woman," Jean said, defiantly, his cheeks turning ruddy and his nostrils flaring. The scar that slashed across his face seemed to glow.

"Yes, but—"

"She was defenseless," he added, as if that was all that needed to be said on the matter.

"I understand, but you killed him?"

Jean pushed up from the table and turned his back, trying to compose himself.

"Was it on account of Catharine?" Magdalena asked, in a small child's voice.

The choked silence that followed told her all that she needed to know.

"Anyway, I have to go to London and face an inquiry," Jean went on, when he found his voice, his back still turned. He took a deep breath and glanced up at the ceiling, as if seeking whatever strength the heavy wooden beams overhead had to offer. "I needed to come home and see everyone before I left, just in case . . . you know . . ."

Magdalena was up in a flash, rushing to him and wrapping her arms around him from behind, pressing herself against his back. She still struggled with the knowledge that Jean had killed another man in a duel, but the thought of stodgy souls on the other side of the ocean deciding the fate of her loved one made her bones run cold.

"We will go with you."

"I won't have it!" he protested.

"Surely they will see what an honorable man you are."

"You are blinded by a love that they don't feel for me," Jean said, turning at last to face her. "You have to understand that my commission is an affront to them—to some of them, at least. Being French, in their eyes, is bad enough. Being a colonial is far worse. It is something less than what they are, the way they see themselves. Some of them, anyway."

"But if they knew about Catharine and how her death affected you, how it affected all of us, and why that might have led you to do what you did . . ."

"You have to understand how far away London is and how someone who lives there sees the world differently than we do. In good times, we timber their ships and sweeten their teas. Our tobacco fills their pipes. Otherwise, however, we are an inconvenience to them, and no one wants to be reminded of something they don't want to think about."

He gave her a lopsided grin.

"Now, I must go," he said, apologetically. "I can't wait to see Pa—and Ma? I plan on giving her a hug whether she likes it or not." He gave a bark of laughter.

They walked arm in arm to the door, and from there, Magdalena watched him cross the yard to the barn, where his horse was stabled. Fingers clawed at her chest. His belongings were still up in one of the guest rooms she had prepared for the seigneur and his daughter, and she assumed Jean would return. But one never knew. She hadn't seen him in ten years, and for all she knew he could disappear from her life again as unexpectedly as he had returned. He might vanish, and this time, she might never see him again.

When evening came, she went about lighting the lamps in her usual fashion. But the house seemed colder now. After the brief interlude of human warmth, it seemed vaster and emptier. Usually, she just lit the lamps in the kitchen and in the room where she planned to read. But now she found herself lighting all of the lamps in all of the rooms, just to brighten the place up. The autumn chill was not very pronounced, but she lit a fire in the fireplace as well, just to watch the flames and feel like she wasn't so alone. With a start, she realized she hadn't told Jean about the seigneur, and she wondered how this could be. How was it she had not shared such exciting news? What did it say about how she felt?

That night, she hardly slept, pulling the blanket over her and then casting it aside, turning from her back to her side and from her side to her belly, flushed with warmth one minute and then chilled the next. In the morning, she thought this would surely be the day Jean would return to the château, and when another day ended with his absence, she didn't know what to do. A wild thought worked its way into her usually controlled demeanor, that she should drop everything and rush to the farm, just to see how her brother was getting on. But she chided herself. He needed time alone with his parents and would have asked for her company if he'd wanted it.

The next morning, she heard a horse in the yard and rushed outside with a cry upon her lips. But it was just the courier from the stage depot in Watertown. Remus bellowed with such ferocity that the young man was reluctant to dismount. He shot Magdalena a look that begged for her help with the dog.

"Remus, enough," she scolded, grabbing him by the collar and holding on. He jerked her this way and that, nearly pulling her off her feet.

"It's just this, ma'am," the courier said, pulling a letter from the leather pouch that was slung over his shoulder. He held it out and she took it with one hand, still holding the lunging dog with the other.

Having left the house thinking it was Jean in the yard, Magdalena didn't have any coins to give the courier.

"Let me go in the house and get something for you," she offered.

"That's okay," he demurred, eyeing the dog nervously. "I'll just be on my way." He dug his heels into the horse's belly and set off at a trot.

"You see what you've done? You've scared the poor boy," Magdalena said to Remus, pulling her canine protector back toward the open door of the château. Once they were inside, she bolted the door, and Remus gave her one of those looks of beguiling innocence.

"Oh, never you mind," she relented, affectionately, as she took the letter into the sitting room.

She sighed from the exertion and excitement of the encounter with the courier, then sat down in her reading chair and composed herself. She assumed the letter was from Lawrence, who hadn't written of late. Her fingers trembled as she opened it and then she just sat there, looking down at the paper, with its ink marks and signature. *Gotzone.* It was a letter from Gotzone, saying that she and the seigneur had arrived in Philadelphia and that she would be at the château in two days' time. Two days? It hardly seemed enough, with Jean's belongings still in one of the guest rooms and with so much uncertainty surrounding his visit. Two days! Magdalena felt as if a bird flew about in her chest, colliding with her ribs.

Now she had every reason to go to the farm to share the news of the seigneur's imminent arrival and to decide what to do about where Jean would stay. But her body wouldn't move. She fidgeted, and then, as the day progressed, she would start one project and move on to another without finishing the first. She wished Isabelle were there to tell her what to do, and then rejected the notion outright, scolding herself for being weak and far too easily led.

Finally, she just waited, and when the second day arrived, she met it with the equanimity of one who has thoroughly rehearsed what she would say and what she would do. Even so, the arrival of the carriage, with its four horses and rattling chains, caught her by surprise, in the way that something that has been anticipated for a long time can seem to happen so quickly when its moment is nigh. Magdalena had put Remus in the mudroom, and his muffled howls spilled out of the house and into the yard.

The coachman leaped to the ground and hastened to the carriage door, twisting the handle and pulling it open. He offered a hand, and white-gloved fingers from inside the conveyance accepted it. Then, a foot descended, a leather pump with stockings and lace, the fringe of a silk dress. The young woman who emerged wore a white cap over dark coiled hair, and the beauty of her somber face made Magdalena catch her breath.

The coachman cleared his throat.

"Mademoiselle du Laux inquires as to whether this is the Château Laux?" he asked.

Magdalena's eyebrows shot up. She said indeed it was, and the coachman climbed up onto the carriage and tugged at one of the trunks secured to the roof. Pushing it past the edge of the carriage roof, he then got down and angled the trunk until he could heft its weight and lower it to the ground. Climbing nimbly back aboard the carriage, he then went after a second trunk.

Meanwhile, the two women faced each other. Gotzone had remarkable poise for someone so far removed from anything remotely familiar to her. That said, it was almost unthinkable that a young woman would have made a coach trip all the way from Philadelphia by herself, for personal safety's sake, not to mention propriety, and Magdalena's gaze stole to the carriage, which sat with its door hanging open. She held her breath, waiting for the long-lost seigneur to emerge, at last. But when the coachman returned from lugging the trunks into the château, he snapped the carriage door shut with a deft twist of his hand, then climbed up onto the bench. With a cheerful wave, he seized the reins and slapped them down on the rumps of the horses, and the carriage jerked forward and then trundled off, leaving the two women standing alone in the yard.

Gotzone's arrival was like a sharp wind that precedes a storm. Her eyes had an arresting boldness, her chin a slight lift that hinted at defiance. There was such a pronounced streak of independence within her appearance that Magdalena could well imagine her making someone like the governor of Antigua uncomfortable, at a time when women were expected to stay in the background.

The visitor rocked back on her heels to look up at the towering edifice. Her brow creased, as if she were weighing thoughts that tugged and pulled at each other. Having crossed an ocean and entered a world that was alien to her in most respects, she appeared to weigh certainty against the ever-present danger of illusion.

"I'm here to see my father's son," she said, with a bluntness that was unnerving. Even in one so young, the rigors of travel had obviously taken a toll. Her face was writ with fatigue, and she seemed on the verge of collapse.

"Perhaps we should go inside," Magdalena offered, ushering the younger woman into the foyer.

"Him in here?" Gotzone asked, the breath falling from her mouth as she looked around.

"Let's get you settled before we worry about anything else," Magdalena said. "I have a bedroom all prepared for you." She hesitated. "Will my grandfather be joining us soon?"

"My father is sick," Gotzone said. "Him still in Philadelphia and say it's up to me. It's up to me to find Pierre. He say this with tears in his eyes."

Her voice splintered and she raised a hand to her throat.

"You must be parched," Magdalena observed. She led Gotzone into the sitting room. "Just wait here and I'll be right back with some creek tea."

"Creek tea?"

Magdalena laughed nervously.

"It's made from the mint that grows by the creek. My mother calls it creek tea. She says it's good for whatever ails you, even if you think you're fine," Magdalena said, flushing to find herself quoting a woman whom she had so often resisted.

Placing a hand against Gotzone's arm, she gave a quick squeeze, then hurried into the kitchen. The jug of tea that she had made earlier waited in the spring-fed cooler, an invention that her husband was particularly proud of. She poured two glasses full of the pale green liquid and carried them into the sitting room. She couldn't have been gone for more than a couple of minutes, but Gotzone no longer waited where Magdalena had left her. In Magdalena's absence, the traveler had found an upholstered chair next to the masonry of the cold fireplace, where her exhaustion appeared to have bested her at last. Her hands lay folded in her lap and her chin rested on a chest that barely moved.

◆　◆　◆

THE NEXT MORNING, A GUSTY wind blew red and yellow leaves past the windows of the house like swirling mobs of brightly colored birds. Magdalena had made a fire in the kitchen hearth, taking comfort from the warmth while she toasted some bread. Now and then, she glanced upward and listened. But the late morning sun was bright against the sitting room window before she heard a stirring from the floor above.

Gotzone came downstairs fully dressed, wearing a blouse with a ruffle at the chest and a full skirt that she pinched in one hand while she held the railing with the other.

"Now we go see Pierre?" she asked, and Magdalena shook her head at the young woman's dogged determination.

"We should have some breakfast first," she said.

"Oh," Gotzone replied, with a fleeting frown.

"We can make it quick. I've already toasted some bread and there's fresh butter in the cooler."

Gotzone looked at her as if the young woman's grasp of English had fled, and Magdalena chided herself for no good reason she could think of. It was just a bit maddening to try to make someone else happy when they were a mystery to you in so many ways, and she hastened to put the toast and butter on the table, along with a fresh pot of black tea. Then, a short time later, the two women sat side by side on the bench of the wagon that bumped and jostled along.

"What is this?" Gotzone asked, pointing at a field of grass stubble.

"That's rye—or what's left after the harvest. Mostly we use it for bread and bedding straw, but it has other uses, too."

"And that?" Gotzone gestured toward a field of yellowed plants that had been bent over.

"We call it Indian corn, after the people who first grew it. Many people feed it to their chickens, though we also mill it and my husband thinks we can expand the market for it in Philadelphia."

"You have Indians here?" Gotzone asked, her eyes widening.

"This used to be their land," Magdalena said, thinking how different the terrain was now than it used to be, and how quickly things could change over time, sometimes in predictable ways and sometimes not. Again, she glanced at her companion, wondering what her presence would do to a family that, up until recently, had not even known she existed.

Gotzone pulled her shawl a bit tighter around her shoulders but otherwise remained silent, and they arrived at the farm soon after. They stopped in at the house first, for it was unthinkable to show up at the homestead and not touch base with Beatrice before seeking out anyone else. But the house was as empty as one of the limestone caves in the nearby hills. Through one of the windows, Magdalena saw Georgie's wife, Rachel, and her little girl, Sofie, in the garden, gathering pumpkins and carrying them to a wheelbarrow. Rachel did most of the carrying, while Sofie grimaced as she squatted and tried to pick one up.

Thinking it best to pursue Beatrice before making any other introductions, Magdalena brought Gotzone out onto the porch. On a farm the size of this one, a person could be almost anywhere, as there was always something that needed doing. But even at a distance, she could see that the door of the chicken house was unlatched on the outside and knew this was where Beatrice must be.

As they neared the chicken coop, Magdalena glanced at her companion. Chickens have a certain smell that seems to ball up in the head, right behind the eyes, but if Gotzone found it distasteful, she certainly didn't show it. Her posture seemed restrained to the point of being wooden, but her eyes were alive, probing and testing, alighting on one thing and then another.

Beatrice must have heard them enter, for she stiffened and straightened up, shifting on one hip as she looked behind her. Her eyes widened. They darted from Magdalena to Gotzone and then back to Magdalena again.

"Mother, we have a visitor," Magdalena said.

Gotzone stepped forward and held out a hand. Shaking hands was not uncommon, as the Quakers often did it as a form of greeting. But usually, it was something that men did, and even then, not nearly in so bold a manner as Gotzone's. Beatrice looked down at the hand and flapped at some straw clinging to her apron, as if she had enough wherewithal to tidy up in the face of the unexpected encounter but didn't know what to do next.

"Where's the seigneur?" Beatrice queried, glancing past the shoulders of the two other woman.

Magdalena hastened to explain that the seigneur was indisposed and that Gotzone was here on his behalf. "We've come to see Pa," she added.

Beatrice seemed to relax, if only a little. Her head moved independently of her body, jerking in the direction of the lower pasture.

"Him and the boys're are mending the fence," she said.

And that was when Gotzone did something that Magdalena would never have expected. She walked up to one of the nesting boxes, where a hen still sat. Sliding her hand under the hen, she moved it about, then held up an egg for all to see.

"Nice and warm," she said.

Beatrice's mouth opened and closed, but she said nothing.

"When I was little girl, we had chickens like these. We had house for them, too, because of the foxes, but not as nice and big as this. It was my job to let them out in the morning and to lock them back up at night."

She placed the egg in the basket that Beatrice held and smiled.

"Shall we go find the person you've come all this way to see?" Magdalena asked.

Gotzone nodded eagerly, and Magdalena took the opportunity to place a hand on her mother's shoulder. Leaning forward, she gave Beatrice a quick peck on the cheek, then turned and left the chicken house with the younger woman in tow.

As they walked down through the pasture, she regarded her companion as closely as she could without being outright rude. The horses kept the meadow grass cropped. But the uneven ground threatened to twist an ankle, and that was when the young woman did another thing that caught Magdalena by surprise. The smartly dressed visitor from across the ocean leaned on Magdalena's arm with one hand and, bending sideways, removed first one shoe and then another. In a fit of impatience, she pulled off her stockings and then gave a smile of satisfaction as she stood barefoot on the rutted ground.

"Much better," Gotzone said, straightening back up again. Still clinging to Magdalena, she carried her shoes and stockings as they continued on their way.

By now, Pierre had noticed them and waited by the wooden fence at the edge of a grove of young oaks with his hands dangling at his sides. Georgie, who had been sitting on a nearby stump, lurched to his feet. He had been watching his older brother, Jean, split a fence rail, and Jean, in turn, dropped the ax-head onto the ground and stood leaning on the handle as if it were a cane. He wore one of Pierre's flannel shirts, along with a pair of his father's wool trousers, and from brightness of his expression, appeared to be fully aware of who Magdalena's companion must be.

"Papa, I have someone you'll want to meet!" Magdalena exclaimed.

A thrush called from the nearby woods and a meadowlark answered from the pasture. The three horses in the field raised their heads as if to bear witness.

Pierre's broad, strong face bore a look of intelligence and curiosity, tempered with caution, that took note of the tiniest detail that his visitor displayed. It was the look of a man who had been disappointed too many times to take anything for granted.

"Father, I'd like you to meet—"

"Gotzone," her companion said, stepping forward and holding out a hand. A trickle of sweat worked its way down her temple, where soft brown curls clung to her skin, but otherwise she appeared in complete possession of herself.

Pierre graciously accepted the proffered hand.

Gotzone squared her shoulders and thrust out her chin.

"My father sent me with important message," she announced, then went on to explain that after many ordeals, including a wooden ship that had gotten blown off course and ended up in the West Indies, the seigneur had reached the end of his tether. Fearing his life was nearing its end, he had sent Gotzone on ahead of him, hoping that through her eyes, at least, he could once again see the son he missed so desperately and the thought of whom had kept the seigneur alive through the darkest of circumstances.

Pierre's eyebrows twitched when she called the seigneur her father, but he otherwise listened with the calm demeanor of the gentleman that he was. The details of the seigneur's incarceration and his subsequent odyssey to reunite with his family were not disclosed there in the pasture, where the autumn sun beat down upon them and barely a breath of air stirred. Those particulars would come later. For now, the business at hand was an awkward encounter between siblings who did not know how, in fact, they were related. It put to the test the courage of a Pyrenean mountain girl who was lucky to be alive in the first place, let alone to be a woman of elevated status, and the forbearance of a man who had every right to hold a grievance.

Pierre's eyes began to redden.

"Enough for now," he said, raising a hand slightly. He turned to look up at the farmhouse on the hill, where he had loved a woman and raised a family on the edge of a wilderness during perilous times. Magdalena could sense his thoughts. She could see them as clearly as pictures and knew full well the pain he carried.

"Let's head on up to the house," he said, holding out his arm to Gotzone. Still carrying her shoes and stockings in one hand, she hooked the other above his elbow, and together they navigated the rough ground.

Now and then, Gotzone glanced up at the towering man and tightened her grip on his arm, and Magdalena felt one of those rare stirrings that might only happen once in a lifetime, when a soul becomes aware that something important is unfolding. Something bigger than any one person. Something one could not have anticipated and yet which seems right and true. Like a story already writ, that had the power to change lives.

◆　◆　◆

MAGDALENA SPENT THE NEXT SEVERAL days at the farm, driving Gotzone back and forth from the château and otherwise trying to stay out of the young woman's way. Gotzone took many long walks with Pierre. At one point, Pierre and Gotzone even held hands, standing at a rise with the cultivated lands in one direction and the tangle of dark forest distantly visible in the other, their figures in relief against the sky. At first, Pierre let it be known that he would travel to Philadelphia with Gotzone, rather than wait for the seigneur to recover enough to come to them. But the family would not be left behind, and it was finally decided they would all form an entourage and travel to the wharf city together.

Even Andrew showed up at the farm with a travel bag in hand. He was Magdalena's middle brother, between Jean and Georgie. Due to Andrew's head for numbers, Lawrence had put him in charge of his first sawmill, and it was Andrew who saw the opportunity to expand and open the second sawmill closer to one of the tributaries of the Delaware River, which offered the power to turn a waterwheel and cut down the number of hand sawyers that would otherwise be needed. While his talent was undeniable, Andrew could be difficult, and he showed up at the farm as contrary as ever.

His introduction to Gotzone went smoothly enough, for a man who openly bristled at the notion of aristocratic privilege and who professed little interest in a land that he considered too distant to be relevant. That said, Magdalena had the sense that he carried a stone in his shoe about something. At first, she thought it was the simple fact that change often led to more of itself, and that Gotzone's presence muddied waters that had previously had the illusion, at least, of being still. But it wasn't long before Andrew sought Magdalena out and put her imaginings to rest.

A series of cold days had come upon them, with a north wind that hinted of coming frost, and Magdalena was in the garden behind the farmhouse, helping Rachel harvest the remaining pumpkins, pluck the tomatoes that still clung to their scraggly hosts, and wrench free the final table corn of the season. She didn't hear Andrew's approach and was unaware of his presence, until he stood at the edge of the garden, watching her labors with a sardonic twist to his mouth.

"It's nice to see you still know how to do a real day's work," he said.

Magdalena straightened her back, grimacing at the knifing pain caused by so much stooping.

"You should come by the château sometime and see what I do," she countered.

Andrew snorted.

"I guess Lawrence has us well trained, doesn't he?"

"What's that supposed to mean?" Magdalena said.

A crafty look crossed his face, and Magdalena had the sinking feeling that she had stepped into one of her brother's traps.

"Well, I mean, there he is in Philadelphia being all high and mighty, while I run his sawmills and you keep his house in order."

"It's my house, too, I'll have you know."

Andrew's face lit up and he raised a forefinger.

"Exactly," he said, wagging the finger at her. "How often does he visit? Once a fortnight, if even that? Meanwhile, you're not only keeping the house but the grounds as well. Whose house is it, really? Does it belong to a man who is too far away to know what's going on, or does it belong to the person who runs it and maintains it and keeps it from ruin?"

"I don't know where you're headed with this, but in case you haven't noticed, I'm very busy at the moment."

"Maybe you'd like to lend a hand?" said Rachel, working nearby, with a basket of squashes at her feet.

Andrew ignored her.

"We're in the same boat, you and me," he said. "Starting the first sawmill was his idea, and I give him full credit for it. But opening the second one was mine, and where is he when it comes to the running of either one? I don't bother myself with the obvious question of why I should turn the profits over to him, when I do all the work and earn the money in the first place."

Magdalena sighed with exasperation. It was always the same with Andrew, the thinking that he was so good at what he did and that no one gave him enough respect. But she feared something was different this time. He seemed to be winding himself up.

"Look, I'll just come out with it," he said. "I'm thinking of opening another mill, only I'm not going to open it for someone who isn't here. This'll be for myself and it means I might not have time to devote to anything else."

"You need to have this conversation with my husband," Magdalena said.

"I'll do that," he said. "I just wanted to let you know first. Because, like I said, we're in a similar situation, you and I. You've got a husband who lives a two-day ride away, and I've got a ghost who owns the businesses I run. We've got to take care of ourselves. We've got to own what's ours."

Magdalena scoffed, but the words pricked. She didn't care what Andrew did when it came to operating a sawmill or anything else. But for him to say that she should declare any sort of independence from her husband was going too far. Whatever arrangements she had with Lawrence were none of her brother's business.

She didn't have much time to dwell on such things, however. Pierre went to Watertown to call on one of the livery stables there. Now and then, coaches could be secured for hire, though coming up with three would be a challenge. In the meantime, Magdalena and Gotzone set about packing at the château. Gotzone didn't seem to have much trouble, as she was used to traveling. Magdalena, on the other hand, was at wit's end trying to fit everything she would need into one trunk, which was no mean feat given that she had no idea how long she would be gone.

Outside the château, Remus woofed, which usually meant a visitor, and Magdalena went out onto the porch to see who it was. Her brother Jean sat astride the horse he had already gifted to his father.

"Is Pa back with the coaches already?" she asked.

She used her wrist to push aside a strand of damp hair that clung to her forehead.

"That's not why I'm here," Jean said.

"It's not?"

"I was hoping you would take a ride with me."

"Now?" Magdalena asked, thinking of all the things she had to do before she could go anywhere.

"I wanted to pay John a quick visit," he said, referring to the Lenape who lived on the estate.

"John?" Magdalena said, frowning as her mind raced.

"You know that after our trip to Philadelphia, I won't be returning to the farm," Jean offered. "I'll be boarding a ship for London, and there's one more thing that I have to do, while I'm here, before I leave. John saved my life years ago, during that militia trip into the backcountry, when I was a kid. I would have been killed if it hadn't been for him, and I have a little something I want him to have."

"Oh," she said, remembering the brooch he had given to her and his gifts to their family.

"He's okay, isn't he?" Jean pressed. "I mean, he's alive and well?"

Magdalena shrugged. "You never know where he is until you see him. He can be gone for weeks or months on end and then just show up out of nowhere."

"You haven't seen him?"

"Of course not," she said, becoming exasperated.

Jean grinned and Magdalena relented, for there was very little she could deny her eldest brother. If they accomplished nothing else, they would at least have the chance to spend some time together, she reasoned, putting aside her reservations and hurrying once again, this time to change out of her dress and into a shirt and a pair of her husband's trousers. Her sun hat was in the mudroom, along with a pair of leather boots suitable for wearing in the woods. By the time she finished, she found that Jean had already saddled a mount for her and waited out in the yard.

There was a time when the wilderness had seemed chokingly near, as if one false step would deliver a soul into the ever-waiting jaws of darkness. Even in the short span of Magdalena's life, however, much had changed. The forest had retreated, leaving pockets here and there, and one of them persisted on the château's expansive grounds.

Riding side by side, she and Jean went down through the meadow. The horses paused to drink at the creek, where the bullfrogs bellowed and the fish that they called sunnies made circles on the placid surface. Redwing blackbirds rose from the rushes along the bank. Mallards winged overhead. John had once said that the trail was an old native pathway, and he should know, Magdalena thought, for his village used to be in a clearing nearby, before the smallpox and measles did their dirty work, and before the nasty business with the settlers, who had no desire to share what wasn't theirs in the first place.

Thinking of John made Magdalena realize how little she knew her husband's friend, even though he had lived on the estate for many years now. The shadow of the forest fell upon them and the woods echoed with the knocking of a woodpecker. Rarely had she ventured past the meadow, and the smell of moss and rotting wood loam clung to her nostrils. Her skin crawled.

John's cabin stood in a splash of sunlight in a small meadow on high ground. It had log walls caulked with moss and a roof of birch poles lying side by side in a manner that would divert rainwater to the eaves. A rock chimney dwarfed the structure. A chair sat along the outer wall, next to the door, allowing an occupant to while away time in sanguine observation of the limited view that the clearing had to offer.

The trail forked, with a fainter one leading to the cabin door, and the deeper, muddier one leading to a corral next to the building. At the far end of the corral stood a lean-to with a manger inside. Several trails left the corral and headed in different directions, one leading into the gloom of towering hardwoods to the north, while others meandered downhill and into the trees to the east and south. The stillness of the clearing was what struck Magdalena the most. The obvious signs of habitation were not enough to overcome the sense that time had somehow slowed to a stop.

"Wait here," Jean called over his shoulder, before swinging his leg back and dismounting.

Magdalena didn't need to be told twice. Jean took a couple of steps toward the house, and when he called out a greeting, his voice seemed to crack the numbing silence. The door didn't budge. Not even a breeze stirred. Jean glanced back at his sister, then helloed again and still received no response.

Letting his reins drop to the ground, he approached the door and knocked. When still no one answered, he gave the door a nudge and it swung inward on its leather hinges. Jean poked his head inside and peered into the gloom, then backed away and returned to his horse.

"We should probably go," Magdalena ventured, nervously.

But Jean ignored her. He opened one of his saddlebags and took out a small pouch. The smell of tobacco leaves left little doubt as to what the pouch contained. Jean gave his sister a brief glance, then returned to the cabin and stooped to enter. A few minutes later, he emerged, pulled the door shut, and returned to his horse empty-handed.

On the ride back, Magdalena couldn't rid her mind of the image of the somber cabin. It seemed to pursue her with silent, padded feet, and her lower belly twisted in a knot. She was not exactly fearful, as her brother was close at hand, but her breath seemed to catch and come up short. Her knees tingled and the motion of the horse agitated her. Again and again, she glanced back over her shoulder, knowing nothing would be there but half-expecting hot pursuit, nevertheless.

When they finally reached the open pasture below the château, she glanced back yet again, and her heart leaped to her throat. For she thought she saw John standing there on the edge of the forest, where the shadows almost obscured him. She was sure it was him, placing the stock of his musket on the ground and now leaning on the long barrel, watching as she hastened up the hill to the protection of the château.

SEVENTEEN

Part of Gotzone's magic was that she could very quickly make you forget that she had not always been a part of your life. She filled a place in Magdalena's heart that had been empty and wanting, and by the looks of it, not only in hers, but in Pierre's as well. By now, everyone knew that the young woman was the seigneur's daughter by adoption, which in and of itself had a certain allure. For adoption may have had a place in the native populations, which had been decimated by European diseases, and to some extent, among the white settlers, such as when children were shuffled off to relatives when parents died. But it remained an unofficial relationship that lacked legal sanction, both in France and the American colonies, which begged the question as to why the seigneur had taken such an extraordinary step.

Answers would be forthcoming in due time, of course. Meanwhile, Gotzone and Pierre became inseparable. Even Beatrice seemed to yield to the young woman's enchantment, and Magdalena felt a twinge of disappointment when Gotzone chose to ride in the carriage with the older couple on the trip to Philadelphia. At least she had Jean to herself, she thought, casting a glance at her eldest brother, who sat opposite her in the rocking conveyance. Once again dressed in his naval uniform, he looked regally distant and far less approachable than when he wore his father's flannels and wools. She watched how the sunlight and shadows that passed through the carriage window danced and played across his face.

In the close confines of the vehicle, their knees nearly touched, and then Jean did the unexpected. He shifted across the aisle to sit by Magdalena's side. Reaching out a hand, he clasped hers, and she pulled it into her lap. For the longest time, they sat with their eyes closed, rocking and jolting on the road rutted with wheel tracks, surging and lapsing as the horses leaned into their harnesses.

"I'm sure everything will be fine in London," Magdalena finally offered, voicing the heaviness on her mind.

Jean's head bobbed, as if in agreement, though it might have been the motion of the carriage. In some ways, he had become a rough and violent man, as his scar and wounds testified. But there was still a soft spot in him that went way back to their youth. He was one of the rarest of men—the kind she could trust with her deepest feelings and most personal thoughts—and she sometimes felt like they were two children in their own secret hiding place.

"There are those who think I should hang for killing a fellow officer," he mused, opening his eyes to peer out the window at the passing landscape. The closer they got to Philadelphia, the fewer woodlots they encountered. The more the land bore the stamp of tillage and habitation.

"Surely they will understand," she said.

"Some will have already constructed the gallows in their minds."

"I cannot even think of such a thing!" she exclaimed, tugging on his hand and placing her head against his shoulder.

He turned to kiss her on the crown.

"I am not sure I would do such a thing again, but I don't regret it," he said. "People have choices in how they behave. Just because a man wears a uniform doesn't mean he has the right to mistreat others he considers beneath him. With rank comes responsibility, and with responsibility comes the need for restraint."

"If they hang you, I will kill myself," Magdalena murmured, meaning every word, for she couldn't imagine living in a world where a man like Jean could not abide.

"You will do no such thing."

"I will, I swear," she said.

"No, you won't," he responded, holding her close as the miles slipped by.

◆　◆　◆

MAGDALENA WISHED THE TRIP COULD have lasted forever, for it seemed too cruel to gain a grandfather only to lose a brother. All too soon, more and more houses clustered along the road, including curious brick structures that sat shoulder to shoulder, with no distance in between. Then there was the smell. The odors of farm country were one thing. One accepted the presence that animals expressed on their surroundings. Harder to accept was the effluence of human beings, with privies that emptied into drainages, and cesspits that tainted the air.

Lawrence met them at his house, which had once belonged to his grandfather, who was one of the early brewers who'd helped to make life in the city more bearable. The man was long dead, leaving behind one of those original log homes that seemed out of place among the newer trends in quarried stone and brick. The small barn behind the house and the rails of the adjacent corral had been painted white in a vain attempt to dress them up.

"Welcome!" Lawrence boomed, red-faced and frenzied at the invasion of more people than the house had seen in its lifetime. He showed them inside, where the hearth had pots that looked as if they had never been used. The walls were bare and there was not enough furniture for everyone. There were only two bedrooms, and it was decided that the men would occupy one and the women the other. Georgie's children could go where they wished, which made Georgie Junior sniff at the notion that he would even consider sleeping with the ladies.

Jean let it be known that he already had a room at a boarding-house, where he had stored most of his luggage prior to his trip to Watertown, and that he would therefore not impose himself on anyone. When he said this, his eyes met Magdalena's. It was well-known that he and Lawrence had their differences, and the look seemed intended to reassure her that any ill will he harbored toward her husband was not a factor in this decision. Indeed, he readily agreed to meet everyone at the tavern where Lawrence had arranged for them to eat that night.

The tavern was clearly not used to accommodating large groups in addition to its other patrons, some of whom had rooms on the premises and others who merely wanted a comfortable place to relax at the end of a long day. It was actually quite small, all things con-sidered, with a massive hearth and a cluster of tables. Lawrence strutted around the dining room, shaking hands and clapping other patrons on the shoulders. He arranged for three tables to be pushed together, and the family sat on benches hewn from logs that had been sawed in half and fitted with legs.

They made an impressive presence, which garnered many an appraising glance. Lawrence held forth on his favorite topics, such as the Scottish immigrants who'd moved into Indian country with little apparent concern for their safety; the increasing calls for mili-tia support as the wildlands became more and more settled; the deaf ears of the Crown when it came to many of the issues that affected day-to-day colonial life; and the Quaker assemblymen, whom he often swore wouldn't shake a penny loose from their pockets if their own lives depended on it.

Meanwhile, Jean, who was dressed in his naval uniform, scanned the room, taking the measure of the other patrons, and more than one person shot a malevolent, unappreciative look back. Georgie attacked the plate of pork ribs in front of him as if he hadn't eaten in a fortnight, and Andrew, clearly out of his element, looked on with sardonic detachment.

Like Jean, Pierre tried to pay attention to what was going on around him. But he seemed distracted, ostensibly by the needs of the women, who were not used to being in a tavern and didn't like the eyes of the men in the establishment upon them. But Magdalena knew it was more than that. She could only imagine how he felt, on the eve of a day he must have thought would never come. It threatened to overwhelm her.

Raising a hand, she beckoned to the server. Normally, a woman would have her husband order for her, and the server glanced at Lawrence. Showing little patience for such convention, Magdalena asked for a tankard of the same libation that Lawrence had, and the server raised an eyebrow.

"You heard the lady," Lawrence said, waving his hand.

The server brought the requested drink, and Magdalena raised it to her nose, sniffing before daring to swallow. The ale's yeasty fragrance was not unpleasant, but the actual taste reminded her of the smell of horse piss, and it took some effort to follow the first sip with a second.

"I want some of that, too," Georgie Junior said.

"We could get him a 'small one,'" Lawrence offered, referring to a diluted beer that was considered suitable for children at the time. He glanced at Georgie, whose mouth happened to be full.

"He's doing just fine with his ginger," Pierre interceded.

Georgie Junior pouted and then sulked all the more, shooting a glance at Gotzone. In fact, he had been acting strangely around the young woman, for some time now, puffing up his chest and putting a swagger in his walk, eyeing her when he thought she wasn't looking.

Meanwhile, Magdalena's ale started to take effect. She normally didn't drink alcohol, declining even the wine that her husband bottled on the estate. On top of that, the ribs that the tavern had to offer were not on her vegetarian diet, which meant that she drank on an empty stomach. The room began to spin, and glancing over at Gotzone, she saw the young woman watching her. Maybe it was the tipsiness, but she imagined they had more in common than not. Upon their arrival in Philadelphia, Gotzone had sent a courier straight away to inquire on the well-being of the seigneur, and Magdalena was not aware of any response that she might have received. All she knew was that there Gotzone sat, along with the rest of them, no better or worse, no more or less, waiting on what the morrow would reveal.

◆　◆　◆

MAGDALENA ROUSED FROM A SLEEPLESS night, as the cold gray fingers of dawn stole into the room. It was the first night she had spent away from the château since moving into it, and the morning chill seemed to enter her bones. The house felt strange to her, even though it was where her husband lived while in the city, and it made her think there were things about him that she didn't know. It was one thing to know he had a life that was separate from hers, but another to actually feel its foreign touch.

Anticipating the family's arrival, Lawrence had secured additional beds, and the sleeping shapes in the women's bedroom were like an unaccustomed terrain, with shape and form that took on definition as the light improved. The spot where Gotzone had slept was empty, and Magdalena felt a stab of curiosity. She got up and pulled on a robe, then tiptoed to the door.

Gotzone was out in the main room of the small log cabin, huddled in one of the chairs with a blanket pulled up to her chin, and emboldened, Magdalena gazed upon the sleeper. A sense of wonder filled her as she looked upon the relaxed beauty of one who seemed so terribly alone in the world that it made Magdalena's chest ache. She wondered what would become of the girl when the man she called her father passed away.

Tucking her chin, Magdalena slipped through the room and out the door, onto the porch, where the cold dawn bathed her face and filled her lungs. The sun was just starting to rise in the east, a tiny sliver peeking above the rooftops. Already, gulls wheeled overhead, uttering their piercing cries, and Magdalena shivered with the undeniable excitement of being in a strange place, with a new day dawning that she knew for certain would be unlike any she had ever experienced. She tugged the collar of her robe tighter at the throat.

Already, the house was coming to life behind her, the murmur of voices, the scrape of an iron skillet on the hearth. Then, the smell of bacon, which made Magdalena's stomach tighten with hunger, even though she didn't eat meat. The hunger that she felt made her wonder why she had pursued such an austere diet these many years now, and she couldn't come up with a good explanation. The Cathars said that meat was an embodiment of the evil that existed in the world, and rather than merely accept such a thing, as she had in the past, she wondered how this could be, that matter could be evil, when it was undeniably a part of who she was and who her family were. The thought tired her mind, and watching the sun climb, she closed her eyes and felt its warmth upon her face.

"There you are," Beatrice said, appearing in the doorway behind her.

Magdalena breathed in through her nose, her head tilting back.

"Best you come in and lend a hand," Beatrice went on to say. "We've got a long day ahead of us and a lot that needs to get done. The men are awake and the children are hungry, I dare say. Do you happen to know where Lawrence is? I thought he was with the others, but they said he spent the night someplace else."

"Yes, Mother, I'm well aware," Magdalena sighed.

"We didn't put him out, did we?" Beatrice fretted.

"Not at all," Magdalena assured her. "Some other assemblyman, who is a friend of his, was out of town and said Lawrence could stay at his house. Lawrence thought it would make it less crowded here, and he was right, no doubt."

"Didn't you want to be with him?"

As simple as the question was, it provoked Magdalena deeply. In truth, it had not even occurred to her to want to be with her husband the night before, when he'd made his intentions known. The thought had not even crossed her mind. Now, she wondered why, and the question continued to gnaw at her as the family ate their breakfast and prepared for the eventful day ahead.

All too soon, the carriages stood waiting in the road in front of the house. "All too soon," because there is something about stasis that beguiles, that lures us into thinking we are ready for whatever will happen next. That we are in control and our past has prepared us for the moment at hand. Pierre seemed calm and composed, but Magdalena was not fooled. She knew how he felt because she felt it, too, coiled in her, like a snake that could strike without warning.

When they reached the boardinghouse where the seigneur was staying, Gotzone quietly took the lead. She did it so unobtrusively that Magdalena realized the young woman had actually been in control all along, bringing the family news of the seigneur, helping them marshal their efforts for the journey to meet him, and now ushering them through the dim corridors of the boardinghouse where he lay. When they got to the room that she said was his, Gotzone paused to face Pierre and hold both of his hands, peering into his eyes as if she could see his soul. Here was a girl who was not even a blood relation, showing them the way, opening the door to a future they might not have ever known without her. She tugged him gently into the room and to the seigneur's bedside.

The rest of the family waited in the hallway, peering into the chamber, holding their collective breaths. At first, Pierre stood looking down at the pale, lined face with the feathered white hair of both pate and beard, the hollowed eyes that stared as if from a distant place, the mouth that worked and the throat that swallowed again and again. Pierre just stood there and then he dropped to his knees, grasping one of the seigneur's gnarled hands and lowering his head to the confluence of bone and withered muscle. Pierre gripped the hand as if holding on to a lifeline, and Magdalena knew it was so, for she felt this too. He was as lost in his father's presence as she often felt in the château—lost and terribly alone. The difference was that Pierre had found something that mattered, at last, while all she had was the ache and emptiness of a hollow space.

One by one, the family entered the room. Jean, who had met them at the boardinghouse, stood behind Pierre with his hands on the man's shoulders. Andrew peered past them, while Georgie stood at the foot of the bed, his arms akimbo. Beatrice stood on the side of the bed opposite her husband, glancing briefly at the seigneur and then fastening her gaze on the one that mattered to her the most, gauging Pierre's mettle and feeding him whatever strength she could. Rachel and the children stood behind Georgie, where even Georgie Junior and Sofie looked on in stunned silence.

Magdalena was the last to enter. As she did so, the seigneur's eyes fell upon her and widened. A light bloomed in them—not the kind of light that shows the way but one that brightens what lies behind, the kind of illumination that is most terrible because it reveals what has been lost. A hand rose from the bed and reached for her. The mouth opened and a sound came out.

"Eleanor!" the feeble voice cried.

Magdalena's legs weakened. She knew who Eleanor was, because she had always been compared to her. The Cathar ladies said she was the very image of her grandmother, and even Pierre had often allowed that it was so. And it was more than she could bear. Somehow, in her search for answers as a child, she had found herself in the grip of an arcane religion, and now, when more than ever she strove to know who *she* was, she found herself trapped by the comparison to someone else. The seigneur grasped with his fingers as she backed away from the bed.

The arms seemed to come out of nowhere, wrapping around her and holding her up. She had not even known Lawrence was present. And yet here he was, like human scaffolding, supporting her, making his strength hers. The rest of the family had returned their attention to the seigneur, who had lowered his arm and now seemed mystified by the hovering faces, and Magdalena had to turn away. She hid her face in her husband's shoulder, seeking the comfort that was there.

"Take me home, please," she gasped.

"Back to the log cabin?"

"No. Take me to wherever it is you are staying. Take me some-place where it will be just you and me," she said.

Try as she might, she couldn't shake a deep sadness, the sense that her life was somehow a lie. The image haunted her, Pierre kneeling at the bedside of the old man, and when she reached the place where Lawrence was staying, she began to sob.

"Dearest, what's wrong?" her husband begged to know.

"What are we doing?" she cried. "Married but separate and alone, and what am *I* doing, clinging to a religion that denies the virtue of living? Where have we gone wrong? What have we done to ourselves? Who have we become?"

Lawrence shook his head, as if to deny what she had said. But no words came from him. No reassurance other than his presence. Nothing about the house they were now in was at all familiar to her. The paintings on the walls were windows into the life of someone she didn't know. The furniture was gullied and worn from the burden of bodies that meant nothing to her. While the assorted cookware at the hearth was much the same as one would find in most houses, the pots and kettles were not where she would have put them. Lawrence took her to the bedroom, where the headboard and quilt were alien to her.

He sat her down on the edge of the bed.

"Tell me what to do," he urged.

Out of earnest desperation, he kissed her on the cheek, and she turned and kissed him on the mouth.

"What're you doing?" he asked.

"I don't know," she said.

Her head swam with images of Cathars who had lived pious lives of restraint and abnegation, their eyes sagging as they gazed at her, their mouths opening with objection. Then she thought of her grandmother, a Cathar parfaite, who had had a child in spite of the faith she professed.

"Please, just hold me," she implored, and Lawrence slipped his arm around her waist and pulled her close. She imagined she could feel every muscle in his body, the breath inside of him, the doubts that must have clawed at him as much as they did her.

"But we had an agreement," he said, with the tone he used when he tried to reason, even when he didn't believe what he was saying.

"I know," she replied, pressing her head against the side of his, and then turning to kiss him again. "But I've been so unhappy for so long," she said, the tears beading and spilling. "I don't know what to do with myself, and now that I've had guests in the château, I never want it to be empty again. I thought I could live with you being gone. I had my books and my meditations, and I thought that would be enough. I thought . . ."

Her breath caught, for now he finally kissed her in return. His hand rose to cup the side of her head and his kisses became more earnest. She lay back and he leaned over her. He kissed her on the forehead and then the mouth. Then, he began to undress her, one button at a time.

She knew he was not the virgin that she still was, for he had been married to her sister, after all. But the fingers that undressed her seemed as unpracticed as hers. They trembled against her naked skin. When he kissed her, he did so with the deference and fear of a schoolboy with his first crush, and later, this was what she thought of—not the increasing haste or earnestness, but the wounded heart of a man who had not been with a woman since his first love died.

✦　✦　✦

Magdalena had only a dim awareness of the days that followed. With his new-found family at his side, the seigneur showed miraculous improvement, and they hastened him off to Watertown. The first snow of the season had come in, with large, driven flakes that whitened roofs and collected in the cracks between the cobbles on the roads. The snow did not have the determined quality of a major storm, but if it persisted enough to cause a problem, the roads could close for days or even weeks, and the family did not want to get stuck away from home.

Magdalena, however, stayed behind, and now clung to her husband's arm as they stood at the wharf, where a schooner awaited the incoming tide. Jean stood with them, watching as the last of the passengers' luggage was heaved aboard, and the face that he turned to his sister brightened painfully. His hug was momentous and lingering. Then, he took Lawrence's hand, with the kind of grip that revealed that past grievances were now forgiven. Jean may have blamed Lawrence, in part, for Catharine's death, inasmuch as one man can blame another for something neither might have been able to prevent. But that was long ago and much had happened since. Their world had changed in a fundamental way.

Jean turned, and as he strode up the gangplank, Magdalena once again grasped her husband's arm.

"What will we do if he never comes back?" she asked, mournfully.

"He will," Lawrence promised.

Jean waved from the rail of the ship, and both Magdalena and Lawrence raised their hands in return. Then he disappeared and Magdalena shuddered. Lawrence slipped his arm around her, and she took a deep breath.

"And now what?" she asked. "Here we are, just the two of us, all alone. What will we do with ourselves?"

Lawrence gave a slow nod, as if mulling the question over.

"I have some thoughts on that," he said.

He glanced fondly at her, blushing, a red apple on each cheek. Magdalena could see the boy in him so clearly that she wanted to protect him for the rest of her life.

"You do?" she said.

"I do," he replied.

"But you have meetings! You have people to talk to and things to accomplish!" she said, catching her breath as she warmed to what she thought he was saying. Hoped he was saying. Astonished that they could actually talk of such a thing out loud and in the open.

"All I can think of is you," he said, with quiet assurance.

EPILOGUE

Jean-Pierre had intended to petition Louis XIV of France for an appearance at court to make sure his land and titles were secure and in order, but though his health was now stable, he didn't feel up to the travel it would have required. That said, he tried to keep abreast of events across the water, and a letter from his sister-in-law, Esclarmonde, put him in good cheer.

Among other things, she shared that she had received a curious visit from a former police *commis* from Toulouse. He had given up police work in favor of the more academic pursuit of uncovering the continued existence of Cathars in the Pyrenean foothills. When asked how his road had led to her door, he related the story of the seigneur that he had found and subsequently liberated from prison. The seigneur had a wife, who had disappeared without a trace, and the commis was convinced she was a Cathar. When Esclarmonde questioned him as to what had become of this alleged seigneur, the commis said that he, too, had disappeared, and Jean-Pierre could well imagine the mirth that must have rippled through Esclarmonde. The fact that the commis who petitioned her was unknowingly surrounded by the very ones he sought would have been the sort of thing that amused her to no end.

She went on to report that François Aguirre had become something of a country gentleman, thanks to the endowment Jean-Pierre had left him. He'd married one of the girls who lived in the same village as he, and in no time, they had a child who they named Guy, wishing no offense to the seigneur, who might have expected the honor. Far from being disappointed, however, Jean-Pierre was delighted. He could imagine his old friend Guy coming to life once again, and it gave him a deep and abiding satisfaction.

As for the manoir, it remained empty for the time being. Esclarmonde now paid for its upkeep, and had installed a marker in the approximate spot where Eleanor slept. Esclarmonde was quick to add that she did not know the exact location of Eleanor's resting place, but this suited her fine. There were some things that not everyone needed to know. As far as she was concerned, Eleanor had a lingering presence that spoke for itself, and Esclarmonde's intention was to preserve the manoir with its mysteries intact and to keep it in readiness for Jean-Pierre, in the unlikely event that he ever wished to return.

Then, finally, she bade Jean-Pierre to hold her in his heart, wherever he might be, expressing herself in such a tender way that he knew Eleanor had to be by her side, guiding her hand as the quill moved against the page. It was a part of Esclarmonde that Eleanor may have known, in her youth, when two sisters were as one, but which he, himself, had never seen.

Finishing the letter, Jean-Pierre folded it carefully and kept it in the breast pocket of his waistcoat. Knowing how unlikely it was that he would ever see Esclarmonde again, he cherished what he had, even if it was only a piece of paper. Inked by her hand, it evoked so many memories that he took long walks on the grounds of the château, which he now called home, lost in dreams of the past.

Against the odds, he lived to be as old as Methuselah, to use Georgie's words. Eventually, he would find a resting place beside a granddaughter and her baby, neither of whom he had ever known but who were a part of him nevertheless. But in the meantime, Georgie's children grew to adulthood. Some of their neighboring settlers might have considered them French, due to the unusual surname they bore, but such roots would mean little to them. Although born in a British colony, they didn't consider themselves quite citizens of the Crown, either. A new spirit stirred in the new land, a restlessness, a sense that something unknown was in the offing.

As for Gotzone, any concerns the family might have had about the legal status of her adoption were put to rest. Jean-Pierre made his intentions clear in his will, leaving her a sizable inheritance, and she went on to live as an independent woman for the rest of her days. Anyone who assumed she had no right to such a bequest was quickly disabused of the notion. Even Andrew had to admit that the family would never have been able to come together without her help, and no one begrudged her the benefits of *hasard*, a French word that Guy Aguirre's son, François, had once taught her.

Her eccentricity lent fury to her endeavors, and with the blessings of Magdalena and Lawrence, she built a whole new wing on the château to serve as a dormitory for homeless girls. When asked why she cared about such castaways, she just sniffed, saying she had her reasons, and before long, Château Laux became a home for girls of any ethnicity or background who had nowhere else to go. She not only fed them and put a roof over their heads, she required that they learn to read and write, as Jean-Pierre, in his time, had required of her.

When such girls had children of their own, the new ones knew nothing of their mothers' suffering. Over the generations, the children of these children knew only prosperity, for Gotzone built a financial trust that sustained them all. Such young women may well have reflected on their patron saint from time to time, fancying

Gotzone to be someone they could have known. Indeed, maybe they thought they did know her, in the way people succumb to delusional relationships of a spiritual nature. But they could never have understood her unless they knew what it meant to be born into a family that sold you to a passing cleric, with whom you lived in servitude until the day you escaped, only to meet a man with ruined health on a dusty road in a distant place. Jean-Pierre had once told her that if she could learn the art of being alone, she could find peace anywhere, and this was a lesson that sustained her through many perilous times and comforted her in a new land that she could never have imagined.

As a final note, it should be added that Magdalena gave birth to a healthy baby girl. If love could spoil a child, then this one was spoiled rotten, for Pierre carried his granddaughter around as if he had grown a new appendage. Though dark-haired, she nevertheless shared her mother's name, and it was said that her feet didn't touch the ground until she was seven, and that even then, her hulking grandfather yielded reluctantly. Lawrence Kraymer retired from the assembly, ostensibly to write his memoirs, though he hardly got past muttering about the Philadelphia Quakers, who in his view were strangling the colony with their self-righteous and parsimonious ways. In later years, as hostilities heated up between the colony and its mother country, the sick and wounded sometimes showed up at the château, where they were attended by an elegant woman with long white hair, who was said to have a healing touch. By then, Jean had resigned from the Royal Navy. Although cleared in the court-martial inquiry that arose from his duel with another British officer, he never forgave the Crown for doubting his honor in the first place. He signed up for a command with the Massachusetts provincials, but that is another story . . . .

Jean-Pierre had once commented that Lawrence's château seemed out of place in the American frontier. Pierre's rejoinder was that the frontier was fast disappearing. The land was changing, the once seemingly endless forest giving way to rolling fields of corn and wheat, and the log houses turning into quarry stone and redbrick homes. Inevitably, the château, itself, changed. It may have had a portentous birth, followed by a tragic youth, and it was bound to harbor more than a few ghosts as the years accumulated. But it had been built to last and was destined to endure for a very long time.

ABOUT THE AUTHOR

David Loux is a short story writer, who has published under pseudonym in *Ploughshares*, *Manzanita*, and other literary journals. At age twenty-two, he ghostwrote a reminiscence of the Holocaust, which haunts him to this day. The critically acclaimed, award-winning historical fiction, *Chateau Laux*, was his first novel, and the first book published under his own name. His second novel, *The Lost Seigneur*, expands on the historical themes detailed in *Chateau Laux* and completes the story of a French family's migration to America in the eighteenth century. David lives in the Mt. Rose area of the eastern Sierra with his wife, Lynn.

ABOUT THE AUTHOR

Jodi Burnett is a Colorado native and a mountain girl at heart. She loves writing Mystery and Suspense Thrillers from her home in the Rocky Mountains, where she lives with her husband and her Rottweilers. There she dotes on her horses, complains about her cows, and writes to create a home for her nefarious imaginings. Burnett is a member of Novelists, Inc. and Sisters in Crime. DETO-NATE is her 20th book along with 5 series companion novellas.